"Kat McGee is a bold, strong heroine and an inspiration to girls and boys everywhere. In this latest adventure, kids not only learn about the history of what America has been but what the future can be with more Kat McGees in our midst."
—Sally Kohn, Political Columnist and Television Personality

"Kat (and author, Kristin Riddick) definitely know their way around a kid's imagination. It was love at first page between Kat and my 9-year-old son, which proved that Ms. McGee can not only hang with the boys but also with any great children's literary character on the market today."
—Nate Torrence, Television and Cartoon Personality

Praise for
Kat McGee and The Halloween Costume Caper

"A wild cross between *Magic Tree House* and *The Nightmare Before Christmas. Kat McGee* is madcap creepy fun!"
—Aaron Reynolds, Author of *Creepy Carrots*

"Kat is a great character for young girls to look to; she faces problems like bullying and feeling insignificant, but she's strong, courageous, and a leader."
—*Sare-endipity*

Praise for
Kat McGee and The School of Christmas Spirit

"Please give yourself a treat and read this book…I'm SO GLAD that I did."
—*I Love to Read and Review Books*

"The seminal work on Mrs. Claus."
—Santa Claus

Kat McGee Saves America

Kristin Riddick

In This Together Media

New York

Illustrations and Cover by Nick Guarracino
Book Design by Makana Ching
Ebook Formatting and Interior Layout by Steven W. Booth

To my history, social studies, reading and English teachers—from St. James (Weathered, Edwards, Todd), to Hamlin (Johnson, Paredes, Hughes), to Ray (Livsey, Peterson, Vaky, Rule), to Virginia (Kett, Howard, Kolb)—You pushed, corrected, praised, critiqued, and inspired me. May there be more of your kind in classrooms today. I hope many enjoy this adventure as much as I appreciate being a part of yours.

CHAPTER 1

SUMMER BUMMER

SPLASH! WHOOSH!

"YIPYEAHHAHHYAYY!" Kat screamed as she flew down the waterslide at Willie Wolleson's Aqua Thrillway water park on Highway 35 on the outskirts of town. Waterslides have a short shelf life in Totsville, Maine, but Aqua Thrillway was close to the top of the list of Kat McGee's favorite things about summer.

And she had a mighty long list.

Besides Aqua Thrillway, summer offered Flag Day in June, three weeks at Camp Cibolo, and family vacations—one time they went all the way to Seattle to see Gram! She also loved lazy days spent reading by Lake Micmac or helping Gram bake her deliciously famous apple pie popovers. But most of all, Kat loved the 4th of July.

Of course, Kat was head-over-heels for all holidays, not just the 4th of July. Valentine's Day was heart-tastic, and Kat loved the funny little leprechauns on St. Patrick's Day. Halloween and Christmas would never be the same after her adventures with Dolce and Sadie Claus. Every time she trick-or-treated or ate a piece of candyfruit she remembered that she, little ol' awkward Kat McGee, had saved those precious holidays from disappearing forever—not bad for an eleven-year-old.

But summer wasn't summer without the 4th of July Festival in Totsville. For three whole days the entire town rallied and played and scooted and celebrated.

It started every year with a picnic and barbeque in Prescott Park. There were games galore—sack races and Chubby Bunny, a hula hoop swirl-off, attempts to squash Jeremiah Blackmon's hot dog-eating contest record (27!)—and bonfires and s'more-roasts. Day two was a citywide baseball tournament (Kat's brother Abe had won Little Tots MVP twice), a tractor pull, and even a home-made ice cream sundae show. Vanilla-peppermint-Oreo with whipped cream and pecans was the perfect end to a hot July day.

But the last, and most important, part of the celebration, the Totsville Parade of Floats and Fireworks (POFF), made Kat giddier than anything else. The school bands were fairly fantastic, and the mayor always looked as if he was having a grand time flashing his smile and waving his hand from the back of a shiny, red, restored Cadillac convertible, but the floats and fireworks that followed were the most spectacular, most splendiferous, most eye-popping events of the entire year! And this year, Kat was hoping to be front and center, helping to direct the entire affair.

Kat McGee spent her early years at Totsville Elementary over-coming an almost indelible nickname, Kat McPee, which she'd picked up after a horrifically embarrassing rollercoaster accident way back in the first grade. Being smashed in the middle of six teasing brothers and sisters certainly didn't help her self-esteem. It wasn't until her magical adventures in Treatsville and the North Pole that Kat felt like anyone listened to anything she had to say. Since then she sometimes felt like she belonged among her ac-complished siblings, even though she didn't have first place spell-ing bee ribbons or violin competition trophies to prove it.

At first, kids at school always wanted to hear about her adventures. She was a grand storyteller and became the center of attention, but she also knew not to get too big for her britches. Unfortunately, it took falling on her face in the Forest of Fear in Treatsville to teach her that lesson. Plus, some kids believed her, but most didn't. Kat saw plenty of eye rolls and heard *liar, liar, pants on fire* whispers, and Natalie Bergeron took it upon herself to spread the rumor that Kat had made it all up.

So over the course of the school year, Kat slowly slipped back into being mostly invisible in the McGee house and at school, which was sometimes okay. Whenever Kat became a tad sad about it, her new friend Anjali Mehta would cheer her up. Anjali loved Kat's adventure stories and often asked her about Dolce or Snaggletooth.

"Wow, Kat. You rode a talking crocodile and outwitted a crazy elf and are here to talk about it! You are super-duper lucky," Anjali would say. Anjali was a good friend who didn't care what the other kids said about Kat. She reminded Kat that she didn't need to be popular to know her adventures were real and true in her heart, and that's what mattered.

But the Parade of Floats and Fireworks was different.

Kat wanted, *needed* to show that she could be in charge and be a leader—not in a magical world that might or might not be real, but right there in Totsville. She was in sixth grade after all; it was time to make her mark. The POFF was her chance.

Kat had volunteered for the parade committee for three straight years, and for the first time ever they were electing a POFF student ambassador to hold a position on the committee and run events at the parade. The student ambassador would be in charge of blowing the trumpet to start the parade, lighting the first firework (just a sparkler, but an honor nonetheless), and supervising the completed float line-up to make sure they were ready to roll. It was a huge responsibility, and Kat knew she was the right girl for the job. Today was the vote, and Kat needed to book it to get to the meeting on time.

Kat jumped out of the pool at the bottom of the waterslide, quickly dried off, and waved to her friends Pearl and Peni, twins from Pittsburgh who were visiting their aunt and uncle for the summer. Kat befriended out-of-towners more easily than kids in her class, maybe because they didn't know about Kat McPee.

Kat threw her stuff in her bike basket and quickly rode back into town, hoping she could beat her thirteen-minute record. Kat wanted a few minutes to practice her speech before the most important POFF meeting ever. This would make or break her summer.

Roman Rule acted exactly like his name sounded—bossy, uptight, and severe. And he was *severely* cramping Kat's summer. *Who has a name like that anyway?* Kat thought, pedaling to the conference room at Town Hall. He was the only thing standing between Kat and her rightful position as POFF student ambassador.

Roman was the biggest bully at Totsville Middle School, but he wasn't your typical mean and tough bully. He was the smartest kid in the eighth grade. Teachers adored him, but all kids feared him. He walked around in perfectly pressed button-down shirts with his nose in the air, portraying the ideal student but acting more like a prickly adult. He was tall and lanky, which only added to his pretentious appearance.

Roman charmed the cafeteria ladies but menaced the sixth graders. He was student council president only because he scared everyone into voting for him. He even had a group of wrestlers beat up Mick Varisco because he didn't wear a "Roman Rules! RULE for PRESIDENT" button. And Kat had been stuck in a room with him all day every first Saturday for three whole months—*gross*.

Kat and Roman were the two student volunteers with the most experience on the parade committee, and therefore the most logical choices for ambassador. They both prepared a written statement to present to the council about why they would make the best ambassador. Then the committee (three members of the Town Council and one teacher) would vote for the first POFF student ambassador. The Town Council members were Georgia Kemp, old man Patterson, and the mayor of Totsville, Leon Little.

Georgia Kemp, married to the wealthiest man in Totsville, was involved in anything and everything that happened in their town. Kat was hoping Mrs. Kemp would vote for Kat because her son Henry played on the same Little League Tots team with Kat's brother Abe. Old man Patterson, whose farm hosted the hay maze and Harvest Festival every year, was a curmudgeon; however, as current hay maze champion, Kat knew she had his vote in the bag.

And then there was Mayor Little. Mayor Little's name was funny to Kat because he was anything but little. He was a larger-than-life African American man, and his booming voice echoed around town as if Totsville had its own year-round Santa Claus. Kat knew Mayor Little would never be as wonderful as the *real* Santa she had visited at the North Pole, but she liked the mayor. Every time he saw Kat he pulled a quarter from behind her ear and let Kat keep it or had a joke that made him chuckle before he finished the punch line.

Being on the POFF committee was cool. The committee designed the floats, ordered the fireworks and decided the line-up, and the student ambassador would help with all of it—how awesome was that? Kat almost dropped out when she found out the ambassador position was between Roman and her; whenever they volunteered, Roman always wanted things done his way. Kat had more experience, but Roman was older and everyone seemed to be mesmerized by his charm, so she had almost quit. Kat's one saving grace was Miss Libby.

Miss Libby was the teacher member of the POFF committee and was the only reason Kat liked going to her social studies class. Her real name was Libertad, which was Spanish, and her dark hair, always pulled up in a bun, sat like a crown atop her head. This, along with her smooth dark skin and twinkling hazel eyes, made her regal and mysterious to Kat. She had a very slight accent that only came out when she was really excited or really angry, which made Kat giggle.

Kat was horrible with dates; her grades in social studies "had a lot of room for improvement," as her mother said. But Miss Libby continued to encourage Kat. She would say, "I promise, one day it will CLICK!" and snap her fingers. Kat appreciated Miss Libby's help, worked hard, and made a semi-respectable B- on her final test of the year. Luckily she was going to have Miss Libby again for world history next year, so Kat really wanted to do better.

Miss Libby claimed history was so exciting that if Kat learned the dates and events that changed America, Kat would feel as if she was magically travelling back to that time. So far, Kat had experienced no such thing. Kat's idea of magic was floating through the air with Dolce and DeLeche, not staring at a chalkboard learning about wars and presidents and speeches. But Kat respected Miss Libby, so she didn't give up on history.

Despite Roman Rule and his tyrannical ways, Miss Libby had convinced Kat to keep her name in the hat for student ambassador, and Kat was so glad she had listened. The floats this year were going to be fantastic, and Kat had helped the committee with them for two months!

The theme was "American Made," and all the floats were going to have famous icons or events on them. The American Heroine float would carry people dressed as Sacajawea, Susan B. Anthony, and Betsy Ross; the Moon Landing float would have a fake meteor shower with sparklers; and the National Park float would have an Old Faithful geyser and Mt. Rushmore carved out of clay. They even had a Revolution float with a Paul Revere impersonator and a real horse! That was a first for Totsville.

Kat was hoping Miss Libby would push the rest of the committee to help Kat win the POFF ambassador position. Miss Libby knew how much Kat wanted it and had secretly told her with a wink and a smile that Kat had her vote.

I am going to win this, Kat thought as she opened the door to the conference room. Then she saw Roman Rule shaking the mayor's hand.

"But I'm only five minutes late!" Kat argued.

"I'm so sorry, Kat," Miss Libby said. "But the mayor and Roman had to start right away."

"But I've been volunteering for this committee for three years! I know everything! He's practically a newcomer!" Kat pleaded. Miss Libby squeezed Kat's shoulder.

Roman looked up and sauntered over to them. "Not to worry, McGee. I'm a fast learner." A fake smile spread across his face. Roman shook his head condescendingly at Kat. "You know, five minutes can be a big deal in fireworks and floats, but I'll be here to make sure you're on top of things. I look forward to you helping me as a student *volunteer*." No one but Kat seemed to notice the snide way Roman stressed the last word.

And as soon as Miss Libby smiled and turned away, Roman leaned down and whispered, "And you'll have to do every single thing I say, runt."

Kat's cheeks flushed crimson, and she turned and ran out the door. She rode frantically home, feeling like fire was blazing out of her ears.

"Roman Rule is a mean ol' jerkypants!" Kat screamed. She wasn't screaming at anyone in particular, but she thought it would make her feel better. She knew it wasn't a nice thing to say, but she couldn't help it. She wanted to wipe that smug smile right off his face with her fist.

"Voting is STUPID! Who wants to be on the parade committee anyway?" Kat growled, slamming the McGee's front door behind her.

Gram ran in to see what was the matter. Since the McGee clan trekked to Seattle last summer, it was Gram's turn to visit the McGee house this year. Kat was glad she was here.

Gram was Kat's only unconditional ally in her family. Ben only liked her when she picked up all his practice golf balls. Her brother Gus liked Kat when the older kids didn't have time and Kat listened to his jokes. Kat knew her parents loved her of course, but with seven kids, they were very busy. It was easy to get lost in the shuffle.

But Kat didn't have to do anything extraordinary or be anything but herself around Gram, and Gram still loved her. She made Kat feel special in a way that no one else could, and it was Gram who knew all about Kat's magical adventures and believed every word she said about them.

Rushing into the house, Kat knew she was upset because she didn't even want to talk to Gram.

"What's the matter there Kool Kat?" Gram loved trying to make Kat feel better.

"I was robbed! I was only five minutes late to the POFF meeting, and they voted without me! I didn't even get to say my speech!" Kat exclaimed, punching the air.

Gram turned to her with sparkling, loving eyes; it was as if tiny bits of happiness jumped out of them every time she looked at Kat. "Why were you late?"

Kat dropped her head. "I was at Aqua Thrillway with Pearl and Peni."

"I see," Gram said. Kat wondered if she heard disappointment in Gram's tone.

"Well, I'm sure Roman will need your help, and this way you'll have more time to enjoy the parade with us! You won't have to worry about the fireworks or the floats. You can sit back and relax." Gram always found a silver lining.

Kat pouted. "What's the point of that? B.O.R.I.N.G."

"Now, Kat—" Gram began, but Kat interrupted.

"Stupid Roman and that stupid vote." Kat threw her backpack down.

"I'm sure there are other responsibilities, and they always appreciate your help, Kat. They must really trust you," Gram said, trying to reason with her.

Kat plopped down on the sofa. "Whatever. I don't want to be a part of it anyway. I'm finished with the committee."

"You're such a crybaby," Emily said, not looking up from her iPad. "Don't be a sore loser." Emily was only a year older than Kat, but ever since she got her iPad she thought she was the bee's knees.

"Shut up, Emily."

Gram put her arm around Kat. "Don't be ugly to your sister, young lady. Emily, no need for sass. I didn't come all the way from Seattle to listen to you girls fight."

"Sorry," Kat mumbled.

Emily shrugged. "Fine. Sorry, Gram," she said, still not looking Kat's direction.

Kat stomped into the kitchen. Gram followed her and started stirring a delicious-smelling apple popover filling. Kat drew in the sweet cinnamon apple scent; Gram's treats were like magical concoctions that made everything better. Then it hit her. Although Gram never admitted it, Kat knew Gram had *something* to do with her magical adventures: the snow globe and the North Pole, the pumpkin pop and Treatsville . . . Maybe Gram could fix it all.

"Can you do something about it?" Kat pleaded with Gram.

"Do something about what?" Gram asked, still stirring her pot of apple filling.

Kat looked around and then whispered, "About the vote. Like . . . magic. Can't you do something to make the committee reconsider? Or make me the student ambassador?"

Gram stopped stirring and took a deep breath. "I don't know what you're talking about, Kat." She shook her head, disappointed. "And even if I did, you can't *force* magic. That's what makes it magic—the surprise, the unexpected, the belief in the impossible and the unknowable, serendipitous circumstances. Like baking, magic is the perfect pinch of a plethora of ingredients stirred together."

In a fit, Kat threw her head in her arms on the table. "You just don't want to. Thanks for nothing." She looked up, immediately sorry she was rude to Gram. But still, she was upset. "Well, you can forget about showing my face at the parade. I won't even enjoy the fireworks!" Kat cried.

Gram tried to be patient. "You know Kat, there is a lot more to the 4th of July than picnics and parades and fireworks. You're missing the whole point! Tomorrow, we'll see if there is some-thing else you can do to help."

"No way! You don't get it, do you Gram? I'll stay home the whole time if I want. I'm tired of everyone telling me what I can and can't do! The election was stupid—I should be student ambassador because I want it more than anyone. Don't you see? Voting doesn't work! I bet Roman cheated. I don't care if there is a 4th of July at all!"

Kat ran out of the kitchen, up the stairs, and slammed the door to her room in the corner on the fourth floor. She fell face down into her beanbag and rolled over as her cats Salt and Pepper climbed up and purred at her.

"If I can't be the student ambassador, I'm finished with the 4th of July. You hear that, Pepper? Finished."

"KAAAATTTTT! Dinner's ready! Hurry up! It's gonna get cold!" Polly screamed from downstairs. Kat heard the triangle her mom usually rang when someone wouldn't come down, as if they were on a ranch being herded to the chuck wagon dinner.

Kat reluctantly moped downstairs. Her brothers and sisters sat at the kitchen table waiting with forks in hand to eat whatever deliciousness Gram had prepared. Kat's parents were away for two weeks, so the McGee kids were getting Gram's royal treatment.

Gram cleared her throat as Kat slid into her chair. "Gus, sweetie, what do you think of when you think of the 4th of July?" she asked.

Gus's face lit up like a sparkler. "That's easy! Fireworks, parades, hot dogs, baseball, your apple popovers—yum! Do we get some tonight? Do we, Gram?"

Gram smiled but didn't answer him. "Okay. Now, Abe, *why* do we celebrate the 4th of July?"

Abe looked around the table. Silence. Know-it-all Hannah raised her hand. She was about to be in high school so she thought she was very smart and very slick.

"Not you, Hannah. I want someone else to answer."

No one moved.

"Emily, who was the father of the Declaration of Independence?" Gram asked. Her voice was soft and sweet, as usual, but Kat sensed a different, underlying tone. Something was definitely up.

Crickets.

"That's what I thought," Gram said, circling the table with her wooden spoon in her hand like a gavel she was about to pound on the table. "I've made a decision. I think you kids are all missing what the 4th of July is really about."

The McGee kids began to fidget and squirm, but Gram continued. "Those things Gus mentioned are wonderful to celebrate on July 4th, but Kat brought up a very interesting point to me this afternoon."

Kat's siblings glared at her accusingly. *Oh no*, Kat thought. *What have I done?*

"So we're going to go on a little road trip. I think you kids need a good lesson in what we are celebrating on July 4th, and why we are celebrating it."

Hannah whined, "But I already know all of that stuff."

"I know you do Hannah, and I'm going to need your help along the way."

"Where are we going to go?" Polly asked.

Gram stood at the head of the table and stretched out her arms. "Philadelphia! I'm going to take you to America's most historic square mile!"

"What is that supposed to mean?" Emily asked.

Gram smiled. "We'll visit Independence Hall, the Liberty Bell, the American History Museum—"

"A museum?" Ben interrupted. "On summer vacation? But the festival! It's only three days before the POFF! C'mon Gram! No way!"

The McGee kids were stunned, jaws dropping to the floor.

Kat shook her head. "Please, no, Gram. Don't make everyone go. This is all my fault." Kat's brothers and sisters stared daggers at her.

Gram put her hands on the table and sighed. "No sir-ee bobtail. I've made up my mind, and, Kool Kat, this is no one's fault. It's going be fun! It will be quality family time we all need before your parents get back and a learning experience to boot. Now finish your dinner, go upstairs, and pack a bag. We leave first thing in the morning."

Kat couldn't believe Gram was doing this to her! She felt so betrayed. She was never going to hear the end of this from her brothers and sisters. This could turn into something worse than Kat McPee.

At 8 a.m. the next morning the McGee kids piled into the family mini-van. With all seven kids, they couldn't even fit in

Gram's station wagon! Kat loved Gram's wagon, which Gram had nicknamed Psychedelic Sally. She had it painted swirls of yellows and green and pinks like a kaleidoscope—Gram was never known for being dull.

Gram pulled out of the driveway and drove out of Totsville heading south. Kat sat in the furthest backseat. She put her head against the window, her earbuds in, and shut her eyes so she couldn't see or hear anything. She wanted to disappear.

But it was easy to hear when Ben pulled her earphone out of her ear and said, "Thanks a lot, Katdog. You're such a summer bummer."

After her crushing loss, Kat didn't think things could get worse. She was wrong.

CHAPTER 2
LIBERTYLAND

McGee family road trips were legendary . . . well, for the Mc-Gees anyway. One time they accidentally left Kat at a roadside gas station in upstate New York for three hours! Eventually Polly noticed that she was missing and the family turned around, but Kat had struck up a conversation with a lady named Dell at the fruit stand and was fine. Kat climbed back in the car with a whole bag of fresh peaches for the family.

During another trip Gus got stuck at the top of the Ferris wheel at Six Flags, and he didn't want to come down. It took six firemen, two trucks, and a crane to get him to the ground safely.

Kat and her siblings would play games for hours, trying to break either a Guinness World Record, like Longest License Plate Game (11 hours, 36 minutes, 23 seconds) or a McGee Family Record, like Longest Breath Held over a bridge (Ben, Penobscot, 28 seconds).

But this road trip was miserable.

Everyone was mad at Kat and on a short fuse. Hannah snapped at Polly and made her cry. Gus and Ben started a shoving match with Abe. Emily was grumpy the entire ride because Gram wouldn't let her text or use her iPad, and then Polly reminded her siblings of all they were going to miss. "Too bad we won't get to see those red, white, and blue sparklers in the shape of a flag. And we'll miss the ice cream contest, and the—" Her brothers and sisters glowered at Kat with every description and scowled.

One look from Gram silenced everyone, but never for long. Almost nine very long hours later, they arrived in Philadelphia. They drove past Independence Park, which was lit with red, white, and blue lights and flew hundreds of American flags, but the museum was already closed. They had to wait until morning.

Normally Kat loved visiting museums. The dinosaur fossils in the Natural History Museum fascinated her, and Kat loved the Craft Museum in neighboring Tradetown, even though most kids her age preferred the Tradetown Arcade. This trip felt more like a trip to the dentist: dreadful. Causing her family to be so upset about missing the 4th of July Festival made it worse.

Kat never thought she would feel this way, but she wanted to go home and hide in her room until this holiday was over.

The next morning Kat and her siblings sat on the steps of the museum with their chins in their hands, waiting for Gram to purchase tickets. The day was gray. Their moods were glum.

"Let's go learn about America!" Gram exclaimed as she came down the steps with their tickets. She acted as if she had finally won bingo.

Why is she so excited? Kat thought. *This is a nightmare.*

Gram handed each child a ticket, but Kat didn't notice until she was almost in the door that her ticket looked different from the others. As her siblings filed in through the grand golden gates and the archway to the first exhibit, Kat inspected her stub.

Shimmering red, white, and blue glitter covered the ticket's edges, and it had a face in the center. Kat looked more closely and saw it was the head of the Statue of Liberty, but she was smiling.

"What is—" Kat looked at Gram quizzically.

"A wise man once said, 'Those who don't know history are destined to repeat it,'" Gram said in her cryptic way. "Kool Kat, I trust you will help when you're needed. Only you will know when to use it," she said, looking at the sparkling ticket and winking at Kat. "Remember, magic is not on demand. It's thoughtfully crafted for a necessary reason, a willing giver, and a deserving recipient."

Kat studied the ticket again. *Help when I'm needed? Magic? A necessary reason?* When she looked up her brothers and sisters were already in the first exhibit, so Kat shoved the ticket in her pocket and ran to catch up.

The McGee kids slowly moped around the baseball exhibit, Abe's favorite. They started there because Abe, the youngest, was known for throwing temper tantrums when things didn't go his way. Covering the walls were framed jerseys and baseballs signed by the likes of Babe Ruth and Joe DiMaggio. Life-size wax figures of the baseball stars stood behind a great pane of glass, holding their bats at the ready, looking exactly as if they were waiting for their final pitch.

"Now isn't this fun? Abe, can you tell us some of the history behind America's favorite pastime?" Gram asked.

"They're just statues," Abe said. Even his favorite icons weren't exciting when they were missing the festival in Totsville.

"Everyone stand back! Please!"

The shouting came from the next room, and the McGee kids ran to see what was causing the commotion. Kat followed her sister Emily into the room labeled "American Revolution."

People crowded around the display case in the center of the room. Guards shoved the museum patrons back, and even on her tippy toes Kat couldn't see a thing.

"Where could it be? How could this happen?" a woman exclaimed beside her.

"They're going to have to call the FBI," another said.

The mob of people was getting bigger and their whispers became louder and more urgent, but Kat was distracted by a pop of light on the wall at the other end of the room, as if someone flipped a flashlight on Kat and then turned it off immediately.

Kat squeezed her way through the crowd and stood next to what she now saw was a door. Kat wouldn't have seen the door—it blended in with the rest of the tiled wall—except for a sparkling, star-shaped doorknob. She hesitantly leaned over and looked at the sparkling knob. It had a slit in the center that looked like a ticket slot. Kat reached into her pocket and pulled out her ticket.

Should I try it? Kat thought.

She turned back to the throng of people, looking for Gram, but the guards were starting to usher the patrons out of the room. Gram had never steered her wrong, but Kat knew Gram was upset with her because of Kat's bad behavior after the election. Was Gram trying to teach her a lesson? Even so, Kat knew Gram always had her back, so what did she have to lose?

A security guard tromped toward Kat, looking like he was about to pick up a stray dog—Kat. It was now or never.

Kat slid her ticket into the doorknob.

Suddenly Kat's entire body was yanked off the ground. Something had a hold of her hand and was pulling her through the doorknob and into the darkness. Kat started to scream, but no sound came out. She saw one huge, red, bursting firework before she landed.

BUMP.

Kat opened her eyes to a room that looked similar to every other room in the museum, except this one had no displays, no art on the walls; it was completely empty.

Kat felt her head, her arms, and her legs. *Ok, no broken bones,* she thought. *That's a good sign.* She was still in her shorts and sneakers, and a chill ran down her spine. Kat had her striped hoodie in her backpack because she was always chilly at the museum, so she pulled it out and put it on over her T-shirt.

Kat stood up and decided to look for her family. Maybe Gram was just playing a joke on her. She turned around, immediately bumped into a large, green curtain, and fell back.

But as Kat lifted her eyes to the ceiling, she saw this was no curtain.

Bright, deep hazel eyes as big as saucers stared down at her. A woman smiled, and her smile looked familiar. But her skin, from her face and neck to her arms, was tinted a mossy green. A halo-like crown encircled her chestnut-haired head, and she held a torch in one hand and a huge book in the other.

She was the tallest woman Kat had ever seen. Her head almost hit the ceiling of the empty room. *Maybe that's why this*

room is empty, Kat thought. *Nothing else can fit!* The curtain Kat thought she had bumped into was not a curtain at all, but a long, green, flowing dress, draped over this enormous robed goddess.

The woman knelt down but was still taller than Kat's dad. "KAT! Finally! What took you so long? I was beginning to think Gram had forgotten about us," she said, breathing a sigh of relief. "But you're here now. Thank goodness!"

Kat was bewildered. "Umm, I'm sorry. But am I still at the museum? And who are you? Where is my family? You look just like . . . " Kat hesitated because what she was thinking sounded incredibly impossible.

The woman smiled. "I'm Liberty."

"That's exactly what I was going to say!" Kat exclaimed. "You look exactly like the Statue of Liberty!" Kat had only seen the Statue of Liberty once from afar on a school field trip to New York City, but it was closed for renovation. Even though Kat had not seen it up close, this woman was a perfect replica . . . except she was no statue.

Kat poked at her dress—it was definitely cloth, not stone. "But . . . but you're alive? You can talk? And move? Where am I?" Kat spit the questions out.

Liberty flashed a perfectly friendly and welcoming smile. "Well, of course I can talk. And I will tell you everything, but we have to go. I must show you what's happened. We need your help, Kat."

Liberty held out her hand. Her face shimmered as if flecks of gold were spread across it, inviting Kat to join her. Kat couldn't figure out why she looked so familiar, but she instantly felt at ease.

Kat remembered how nervous she was when she first arrived at the School of Christmas Spirit, but Sadie Claus had immediately made her feel welcome. Then she thought of how safe she felt floating with Dolce out of the magic pumpkin patch. She certainly wasn't going to stay in this dark, quiet room alone, not knowing how to get out or where her family was. She reached up and put her tiny hand in Liberty's giant palm.

Here we go again! Kat thought . . . and for the first time in two days, she smiled.

Liberty held her torch out in front of them, and an invisible force started pulling them in whatever direction Liberty pointed it. The torch guided them out of the empty room, and the giant green woman and small curly-haired girl stood at a doorway to what looked like a normal museum display with baseballs and trophies. Kat almost said she had just left the American Baseball room, but she kept her lips sealed. Liberty looked at Kat with a mischievous smile as they took a step inside.

At first glance, Kat thought the room was the same. She was about to tell Liberty how much Abe usually loved this room, but as she looked more closely, Kat realized there were no framed jerseys or huge replicas of baseball legends or glass-encased autographed baseballs.

Everything in the room was moving.

Babe Ruth was talking to Joe DiMaggio, who stood in the same stance with his bat that Kat had seen earlier, except now

Babe appeared to be giving Joe pointers on his swing. Willie Mays and Ty Cobb were eating hot dogs on a set of bleachers with Jackie Robinson. When Liberty and Kat entered, they all looked up and waved hello.

The room seemed to extend as far as Kat could see; she couldn't figure out where it ended. As soon as they stepped in the door, the walls disappeared! Hank Aaron was hitting baseballs in a batting cage. A group of ladies in old-fashioned uniforms were playing on a baseball diamond. Kat was so confused.

Liberty explained, "Oh, those are the women from the All-American Girls Baseball League. It was only around during World War II when the men were off at war."

Kat remembered that from a movie her parents liked. But that wasn't why she was confused. "Are they mannequins?" Kat asked. "Or robots? Or actors?"

Liberty threw her head back and laughed. "Oh, no, Kat. They're the real deal. Welcome to Libertyland . . . a living museum of America."

Kat shook her head. "*Living* museum? What does that mean?"

"Exactly that. Everyone's alive. We have the greatest events, icons, foods, music—we have everything that is unique and interesting and amazing about America."

Kat didn't fully understand until Liberty's torch led them from the baseball legends through each doorway. In the Wild West room, Will Rogers talked to John Wayne, and Gene Autry and Buffalo Bill rode horses around a corral.

They passed through Apple Pie Plaza where shelves of apple pie were stacked as high as a tower, and in the center of the room families sat around a huge round table, the size of a swimming pool, that held one humungous apple pie.

Liberty swept them through the Moon Room, where Neil Armstrong, Sally Ride, and other astronauts floated around in the air as if they were in space, and as soon as Kat stepped into it she started to float too! No gravity! Cool!

In every scene they passed, Liberty was like the disco ball in the room—shining and spinning around so she could say hello to everyone. Every person gravitated toward her to be near the effervescence and energy Liberty radiated. She could make a room quiet with one look or light it up with her laughter. *No wonder everyone wants to be near her*, Kat thought. *She immediately makes everyone feel at home.*

As Liberty led Kat through each room, or area, or miniature world, or whatever it was, another doorway would appear out of nowhere. As soon as they stepped through, they were in a normal hallway again, as if the museum had suddenly reappeared.

They passed Amelia Earhart and the Wright Brothers tinkering with some airplanes; country music legends Patsy Cline and Hank Williams were singing with a band in one room, and Sacajawea was building a fire with Lewis and Clark in another. Hamburger Heaven made Kat's mouth water: Hamburgers, french fries, and milkshakes were everywhere!

Liberty's pace quickened and Kat couldn't look into every room. Kat tripped, but Liberty held her up to keep her from falling.

"I'm sorry to rush, but something is terribly wrong in the Revolutionary War room. This is why I sent for you, Kat." Her tone was urgent and somewhat intimidating.

Kat was nervous again. "Wh-wh-what's wrong? Why do you need me?"

Liberty turned and managed a small smile. "Don't worry. We're almost there." Kat wasn't encouraged.

With that they whipped around a corner and through a doorway marked "The American Revolution." Instead of stepping into a magical and dynamic miniature world like the others, Kat only felt a somber, quiet sense of urgency when she walked over the threshold.

A man in a funny looking costume and white curly hair (or was it a wig?) ran to Liberty. "What took you so long? Vanished! Both of them! And with only two days! We're doomed!"

Liberty's voice was serious but calm, and her face was stoic. "John, relax. Tell me exactly what happened, and we will figure out what to do." A group of men with the same short knickers, tights, and long tailcoats gathered around them.

The man began pacing in front of them as if he was about to give a speech. "I declare we do not know, dear Liberty. We know that Mr. Jefferson was at one moment here among us, and the Declaration in its holding case. We prepared our presentation for the anniversary of the signing two days hence. And the next moment both he and the most important document of our time had vanished into thin air, as an apparition is wont to do."

"Astonishing!"

"I have never seen such a thing!"

"God help us!"

"Inconceivable!"

"The British are behind it I am sure of it!"

They sure do talk funny, Kat thought.

Kat turned away from them and couldn't believe her eyes. There, in front of her, was her family—staring right at her.

The McGee kids and a throng of people were on the other side of what looked like a long plate of glass, just like the one she had seen earlier in the baseball room with Abe.

Kat ran over to it and waved. "Hey! You guys would love this! Can you see me? Can you hear me?"

"Don't be absurd, lassie," the man in tights said.

Kat's family didn't move. No one moved. They stood frozen, staring down at an empty glass case, much like the one right in front of Kat now. *They look like . . . like . . . statues,* Kat thought.

"Are they ok? What's going on?" Kat was worried.

Liberty walked over to Kat and said reassuringly, "There is nothing to be scared of. They are fine. If you were there, you would see figures and statues on this side of the glass. But you're in the Living Museum now, so you see the museum and everyone in it from our point of view. It's different here. We can move and breathe and talk. You're on the other side, Kat. Think of it as the flipside of what you're used to seeing."

Kat was not convinced.

Liberty took Kat's hand. "I promise you that your family is safe. They don't even know you're gone."

Kat didn't fully understand what was happening, but as long as her family was okay, she decided not to argue but to get answers instead. "Why am I here?"

"We need your help. Did you understand what Mr. Adams was saying?"

"He was talking so fast I just got pieces," Kat said, trying to look away from the throng of people, including her family, who were frozen like statues. "But someone named Jefferson is missing. With something important?" She looked questioningly at Liberty.

The man ran and stood directly in front of her. "Dear child, 'Someone named Jefferson' happens to be Thomas Jefferson, statesman, orator, and author. That 'something important' changed the entire course of history! That 'something important' declared that all men were created equal! That we all have the right to life, liberty, and the pursuit of happiness! That 'something important' created democracy! That 'something important' is none other than the DECLARATION OF INDEPENDENCE!"

Silence fell over the room.

Kat felt as if her eyes were about to pop out of her head. *Jiminy!* She thought. *He sure is worked up. I didn't realize he was talking about THE Thomas Jefferson and THE Declaration of Independence.* She had just learned about them in Miss Libby's class last year.

Liberty knelt so she was closer to Kat. "What Mr. Adams is trying to say, Kat," she calmly continued, "is that Thomas Jefferson and the Declaration of Independence are missing. And if they're missing from here, that means they are also missing in their most important moment in history. For Mr. Jefferson and these people," she motioned around the room, "that was July 4th, 1776. That was the day the Declaration of Independence was signed by all the members of the Continental Congress during the American Revolution. That was the day the United States of America was created—the very first 4th of July."

Kat shook her head, unsure of why she would need to be a part of this.

Liberty continued, "If Mr. Jefferson isn't there to present the document that he wrote for all of these men, the members of the Continental Congress, then the United States will disappear. No one knows what kind of impact that would have on our history as a nation, because the nation won't exist."

Kat was shocked. She knew the Declaration of Independence was important. And she knew Thomas Jefferson was a big wig and a President of the United States. But she didn't know there *wouldn't be a United States* without him.

"Who would want to kidnap Thomas Jefferson and take the Declaration of Independence?" Kat asked, looking around at the strange men.

"Child, at that time, in that place, the list . . . is endless," John Adams said, shaking his head.

Liberty stood up. "This is where I can help, and why I asked for Kat. I think I know who did it. And I think Kat can find him and bring Mr. Jefferson and the Declaration back."

The crowd of people turned expectantly to Kat.

Kat tried to swallow, but she had a lump in her throat the size of Totsville.

CHAPTER 3
LIBERTY'S LOOKING BELL

Liberty pulled Kat out of the American Revolution room before anyone could stop them, promising the scared and emotional mob that they'd soon return.

Kat opened her mouth to argue, scream or otherwise tell Liberty she must be joking, that maybe Kat should turn around and find Gram and her siblings. No words came out, but her mind was racing: *What in the world could she want me to do? Why would I be able to find Thomas Jefferson? And the Declaration of Independence? That's too much pressure—I'm not even twelve yet! And didn't Liberty say there was a WAR going on? Oh, Gram, why did you send me here?*

Liberty's torch was pulling them magically up a winding staircase. Up, and up, and up. Kat felt like they couldn't possibly still be in a building when they stopped in what looked like a tower.

Kat looked around and all she could see were stars—no buildings, no land, no roads or cars—just stars.

"Wow," she marveled.

"Oh, this? Yes," Liberty said. "I see a great deal of good and bad up here."

"What do you mean?" Kat took a step back, bumped into something that startled her. She turned and a grand, luminous, glowing bell was three inches from her. It was almost as tall as Kat—if it were upside down she could probably fit inside of it!

Kat reached to touch it, and her hand bounced back. It wasn't quite a shock, but the bell felt somehow full of energy—it was almost pulsing and vibrating. It felt a little bit like the foot massage thingies in the mall in Totsville. She put both hands out, and she felt that energy massage again. Weird!

"What is this?"

Liberty stepped up beside her and placed her hands on the bell. "It's my looking bell."

"A looking bell? What does it do?" Kat asked.

"The looking bell is my way of seeing and ringing in all that is good, and bad, about the past, present, and future of America," Liberty said with pride.

Kat was still confused.

Liberty continued, "Let me show you. Unfortunately, because of the situation in 1776, the future looks bleak." She took a step back and pointed her torch at the bell, and commanded,

OH BELL OF MINE YOU RING SO FREE
SHOW US WHAT THE FUTURE WILL BE.
WITH NO JEFFERSON OR DECLARATION TO SIGN,
PAINT A PICTURE OF JULY 4TH 2029!

The bell shined brighter and rang three times, and the outside of the bell became a canvas of fireworks. Red and green and blue and purple sparks shot in different directions, and each spark became a part of a picture, as if the entire bell was a photograph.

The image on the bell started to move, and it was as if Kat was watching a silent movie in front of her.

Kat was shocked at what she saw on Liberty's looking bell. If this was supposed to be July 4th, 2029, something was definitely wrong.

No parade or picnics were in this July 4th celebration. No red, white, or blue streamers decorated the streets. In fact, there was not really color anywhere. Everything from the buildings to the cars to the clothes people wore was a dull gray color. As each image popped up on the bell, Kat saw signs that said "RULER-WORLD".

People wore RULERWORLD uniforms: gray pants and a white shirt with a RULERWORLD patch. Cars were all RULER-ROLLS vehicles. The movie theatre said RULERWINK CINE-MA showing a movie called "The Ruler Games." RULERWINK COFFEE AND TEA was on a corner, and the gas station was called RULER GAS. Kids walked to RULERWINK ELEMEN-TARY, and adults shuffled in to RULER WORKS FACTORY. Trash littered the streets, and cars almost ran into each other at every intersection because there were no traffic lights or lanes.

Kat shook her head, confused. She looked at Liberty. "What is that place? Those people look so angry and sad."

"That is Totsville on July 4th, 2029," Liberty said sadly. "Only it's not Totsville. It's Rulerworld."

Kat saw a gray flag with a black "R" in the center. The same flag was on every building and every street sign. "But that can't be Totsville. And that certainly can't be the 4th of July. Where's the parade? The celebration? The fireworks?"

Liberty's face was still. "That's just it, Kat. There is none of that in the future, because no one in 2029 will celebrate the 4th of July. Because of Rulerwink, the holiday doesn't exist."

Kat was frozen. She blinked, and stared at the bell. "I . . . I don't understand. What's Rulerworld? Who is Rulerwink?" Kat asked.

Liberty sighed. "I believe he is the one who has kidnapped Thomas Jefferson and stolen the Declaration of Independence. This is what will happen if he succeeds in keeping them until the 4th of July.

If Thomas Jefferson doesn't get the Declaration of Independence back to be signed, then the Revolutionary War won't have happened. There will be no 4th of July, no independence, no freedom. Kat, there will be no United States. That means there is no democracy—no elections, no freedom to choose who leads the country, no president. Rulerwink must have stepped in and created his own country: Rulerworld."

"Do you know how this happened? How did Rulerwink get away with it?" Kat asked.

Liberty tapped the looking bell once more with her torch.

OH BELL OF MINE SHOW US THE PLACE IN TIME,
WHERE THINGS WENT WRONG IN THIS MIGHTY CRIME.
IF WE ARE TO FIND THEN WE MUST FIRST SEE
WHERE TJ AND THE DECLARATION MAY BE.

The fireworks again exploded in a blast of color, and a picture appeared of a man in tights and knickers tied to a chair in what looked like a log cabin. A tall, dark shadow was in the corner of the cabin's one room. Kat couldn't make out his face, but a black "R" was on the pocket of his gray jacket. An hourglass and a candle were on a table in the center of the room, a tattered and torn flag was hanging in the opposite corner, and a giant star-like carving was in the wall. The man in the chair with his hands tied looked scared.

Liberty explained. "The bell can only show us certain moments, but Thomas is definitely in trouble. John Adams told us the incident just occurred, so Rulerwink must have kidnapped him today, the second of July . . . but July 2nd, 1776."

"But if all of that happened 1776, how are we supposed to do anything about it *now*?" Kat asked.

Liberty turned to Kat. "You'll have to go back."

Kat did not believe her ears. "Back *in time*?!"

"That's the only way. We need to make sure Mr. Jefferson is returned and the Declaration is signed by the 4th," Liberty said.

Kat relaxed slightly. "We? So you'll be going with me, right?"

"Kat . . . " Liberty started.

Kat didn't like the tone in Liberty's voice. It sounded like she was about to tell Kat her dog had died or she had fourteen cavities.

"Kat, look at me. I look like the Jolly Green Giant. You think I'll be able to blend in if I suddenly arrived in 1776? Not a chance!"

Kat thought about this. Liberty was right. She would stand out like a sore thumb anywhere she went, but especially in the middle of the American Revolution.

But there was a bigger issue. Kat looked out from the tower into the starry night. She didn't see anything that would help.

"How exactly am I supposed to go back to 1776? I don't see any time machines around here." Kat immediately regretted her hotheaded, snarky tone and felt as if she had snapped at Gram all over again.

Liberty dropped her head, disappointed.

"I'm sorry. I don't mean to be impolite," Kat said apologetically. "You obviously have . . . some kind of magic powers, and a really cool magic torch. Maybe I still don't understand exactly what's going on, but sending me back in time seems a little crazy. And a little impossible."

Liberty raised her head. "It is a little crazy. A little improbable, maybe, but not impossible. When I heard what you had done in Treatsville and at the School of Christmas Spirit, you sounded like a girl who would be up for the task. I thought you would at least be willing to try."

Kat didn't know what to say. This was the history of the United States they were talking about. What if she did something wrong and changed the course of the country forever? Or worse, what if she failed? What if she walked out of this magical living museum to a world like Rulerworld? She was horrible at history! She really didn't want to screw it up for everyone.

Liberty continued, "I have a way that might work, but only if you understand the importance of what you're doing, of what you're saving. Do you fully comprehend what Rulerworld would be like? He would not stop with the Declaration of Independence. He will take away America's identity, one icon at a time. We will lose everything we hold dear, from baseball to apple pie. Everything and everyone in those rooms we passed will disappear forever."

Kat shivered.

Liberty reached down and touched Kat's shoulder. "I know it's hard for young people to understand the importance of freedom, but it is too dangerous for someone who isn't wholeheartedly committed. This is a responsibility not just anyone could take on. Was I wrong to think you could?"

Kat was quiet and still. She looked out into the stars and hoped for an encouraging word from Gram or a nudge from Miss Libby. Then it hit her.

Miss Libby!

Liberty reminded Kat of Miss Libby! Liberty's green tint was a lot different from Miss Libby's smooth brown skin, but the green eyes and friendly smile were the same. That's why Kat felt so comfortable the minute she was pulled through the doorknob and arrived in this strange living museum. Kat also remembered that Miss Libby's real name, Libertad, was Spanish for "freedom."

This must be a sign! Kat thought.

Kat recalled Miss Libby's encouragement whenever she struggled with history and dates. Miss Libby believed Kat could do better, that she was smart enough to improve. And Gram always saw the good in Kat, even when she was a sore loser. Kat remembered Gram's words: *I trust that you will help when you're needed.* Kat knew what Miss Libby and Gram would want her to do.

Kat thought about what Liberty said. She didn't know if she fully grasped the importance of democracy and freedom. She knew that democracy meant that the people were able to choose the government through elections, just like the committee chose the POFF chair and the students of Totsville Elementary chose the student council president. *Ugh. And nasty Roman Rule won BOTH of them*, Kat thought. *I don't care if those two elections disappeared.*

But where would they be without the president of the United States? She wasn't sure she knew the answer, but she knew two things for certain:

One, Rulerworld looked horrible. She would never want to live in a place where everything and everyone looked the same, moped around miserably, and didn't know what the 4th of July or a president was. If the world without elections and democracy and freedom looked like Rulerworld, then she knew they were necessary.

Rulerwink reminded her of rotten Roman Rule. He probably would do something awful like kidnap Thomas Jefferson and steal the Declaration of Independence. Plus, she would NEVER want to have to do what Roman said every day for the rest of her life.

Secondly, Liberty needed her help. If Kat had not helped Dolce because she was nervous or not ridden the sleigh because she was scared, none of those adventures would have happened! She never would have been able to meet Cookie Crocodile in the Swamp of Sorrows. She and Sadie Claus never would have saved Santa from Scoogie sending him to the South Pole!

Liberty's looking bell glowed in front of Kat, shining brightly and showing her a time and a place that looked strange and weird and completely foreign. She swallowed hard and turned to face Liberty.

In the glow of the looking bell, Kat said as confidently as she could muster, "So, how does a girl from Totsville find her way to 1776?"

CHAPTER 4

THROUGH
THE CHALKBOARD
OF CHANGE

Liberty's torch guided them down the tower stairwell away from the looking bell, through several dark hallways and across another threshold. This room did not open into a miniature world like the others Kat had seen; it looked almost like an ordinary classroom. The difference was that the walls were covered in not one but hundreds of chalkboards, from floor to ceiling, all shapes and sizes.

Kat and Liberty walked the length of the room, and Kat stared at the walls in front of her. Each chalkboard had a date or an event listed on it. Some of them Kat recognized, and some were completely foreign:

1492: COLUMBUS SAILED THE OCEAN BLUE

That one is easy, Kat thought.

DECEMBER 7, 1941: A DAY WHICH WILL LIVE IN IN-FAMY

"What does *infamy* mean?" Kat asked. She didn't know that one.

"It means it is famous for something bad that happened. Infamous means that everyone knows about it, but not for how great or special it is, but how bad it is. So everyone will remember that day because of the bad thing," Liberty explained.

Okay, Kat thought. *I guess that makes sense.* Before Kat could ask Liberty what happened on that day that was so horrible, she saw a good date:

JULY 17, 1955: DISNEYLAND OPENS

Fun! Rollercoasters! Rides! Shows! I want to go to Disneyland! Kat thought.

They passed more dates on more chalkboards. Some of them were interesting:

AUGUST 18, 1920: WOMEN GET THE RIGHT TO VOTE

Some were sad:

APRIL 15, 1865: LINCOLN ASSASSINATION

SEPTEMBER 11, 2001: WORLD TRADE CENTER ATTACKS

Some of them Kat were familiar because Kat had studied them in school:

DECEMBER 16, 1773: BOSTON TEA PARTY

But some of them Kat didn't recognize:

1692: SALEM WITCH TRIALS

Kat wanted to know more about that one. She would have to remember to ask Gram when she got home.

But then the dates all started running together, and Kat remembered why her grades weren't so good in history. Her head started to spin. **1607: JOHN SMITH FOUNDED JAMESTOWN. MAY 17, 1954: BROWN VS. BOARD OF EDUCATION DECISION. FEBRUARY 23- MARCH 6, 1836: BATTLE OF THE ALAMO. OCTOBER 29, 1929: STOCK MARKET CRASH.**

"There's so many of them! What do they all mean?"

"They're all important dates in American history, when an event or person or thing made a big impact on our country. In Libertyland we like to call them the chalkboards of change. We all learn something when we step in here."

"But how are they going to get me back in time? What do these have to do with 1776 and Thomas Jefferson and the Declaration of Independence?"

Liberty smiled. "I'll show you." She grabbed Kat's hand and walked to the nearest chalkboard. It read:

AUGUST 15-18, 1969: WOOSTOCK FESTIVAL, THREE DAYS OF PEACE AND MUSIC

"Have you heard of Woodstock?" Liberty asked.

Kat nodded. Kat had seen a Woodstock T-shirt with a peace sign on it at the arts and crafts fair she went to every summer in Totsville. This year Gram had arrived on the day it opened and had taken Kat to the fair. Kat had never heard of Woodstock and asked Gram what it was.

Gram told her all about the music festival in a huge field in New York. Gram said it was full of long-haired hippies and rebellious teenagers who had walked or hitchhiked more than a hundred miles to get there! Kat remembered asking, "Did you walk a hundred miles, Gram?"

Gram had smiled and her eyes seemed to go to a faraway place. She looked at Kat and said, "You know Kool Kat, I wasn't always this old and slow. I could really shake my bootie!"

Kat had laughed so hard at Gram dancing around the fairgrounds. Some days Kat had a hard time walking to school so she couldn't imagine walking a hundred miles just to listen to some music! It was because of Woodstock that Gram had painted her wagon and named it Psychedelic Sally years later.

Liberty snapped her fingers and said, "Okay. I want you to stare at the board and concentrate on what you think 'three days of peace and music' would be like. Really think about it."

Kat thought about Miss Libby trying to get her to concentrate on the dates in history class. Miss Libby had said if she did that, she would magically be transported to that time period in her mind. Kat was pretty sure this wouldn't work either, but she decided to try. Liberty did have a magic torch after all.

Kat stared at the date on the chalkboard for a couple of minutes, but it felt like an hour. And then something really weird started to happen. The board made ripples, like the water did when she and Anjali skipped stones in the lake behind Anjali's house just two weeks ago. She leaned closer and heard music playing and people laughing. Kat looked around the room to see if anyone was there, but it was just Liberty and a bunch of chalkboards.

"What's going on? Are you playing a trick on me?" Kat looked at Liberty suspiciously.

Liberty smiled. "Concentrate."

Kat looked back at the board, and then reached her hand out and put her fingers to the chalkboard and touched it.

WHOA!

Kat jumped back, startled. Her fingers had sunk into the chalkboard like it was made of goo! It was soft and felt like those squishy balls that squeeze into all different shapes and sizes but then bounce right back to a ball. She thought that her hand would certainly be wet or slimy when she pulled it out but it was completely dry, as if nothing had happened.

She looked at Liberty. "What was that?"

"That's what the chalkboards of change can do. If you think about what's written on them long enough, they can take you back to that time."

"You mean Miss Libby was right? But . . . " Kat wanted to know more. She wanted to go through them all! Like the day *Sesame Street* first aired. Or the day the Wright Brothers flew their first plane.

"Let's go! Let's start here! I want to go to Woodstock!" Kat screamed, forgetting for a moment why she was there.

Liberty's smile faded. "There won't be a Woodstock if we don't get you back to 1776. Now, where is that board?" Liberty scanned the room. "Aha!"

Kat followed Liberty to the other side of the long, narrow room, but it seemed to be getting longer and longer as they walked. Where did this place end? More chalkboards and more dates. Kat was so curious about all of them!

Liberty stopped in front of the board that read:

JULY 2, 1776: THE VOTE FOR INDEPENDENCE

"But that's not the 4th of July," Kat said, confused.

Liberty explained, "No, this is when the group of men voted for independence from Britain. Since today is July 2nd, it is also when they realized Mr. Jefferson and the Declaration were missing. You will have two days to find Rulerwink and hopefully discover the hiding place. You must rescue Mr. Jefferson and find the Declaration of Independence so that it can be signed on the 4th. Otherwise . . ." Liberty trailed off, looking away.

Kat gulped. She didn't want to think about what would happen if she failed.

"You sure you can't come with me? Can't you just hide somewhere? How am I supposed to find them? I'm not sure I can do this alone!" Kat was frightened and nervous.

Liberty put her hand on Kat's shoulder reassuringly. "You will not be alone." Liberty then took her torch between her hands as if she was trying to squeeze it together, and it shrunk down to the size of a flashlight. She handed it to Kat.

"May it light your way when you need it the most," Liberty said. "It will show you the path if lost, shine the light if darkness overcomes, make the impossible seem possible, and point the way home when you're ready." She continued, pleading, "We need you, Kat McGee. We need you to save our beloved country and our favorite holiday."

Kat took the tiny torch and put it in the safest compartment in her backpack. She turned and stared at the chalkboard in front of her. *Ready or not, 1776, here I come!*

The floor of the cabin was dusty, and Thomas was worried. He was trying not to let this madman know that he was scared, because he still hoped Mr. Adams, Mr. Hancock, and the rest of the congress could join forces to find him. He decided to be calm and polite, and hope that reason would prevail.

"Dear fellow, you are making a mistake. I urge you to reconsider. Perhaps you do not realize what is at stake?" Thomas looked at the tall, skinny young man in the corner.

"Oh, Mr. Jefferson, I know exactly what I'm doing. Do you not think that I am aware of your stature and importance?" the man with the long angular face walked closer and put his monocle on as if he were examining a patient. "Why do you think I chose you? *You* are the one who will help me! If they think you are on my side, nothing can stop me—even this silly piece of paper."

They both looked at the Declaration of Independence on the table in the corner of the small room, next to several pots of tea.

The man walked over to it and stroked it with his bony, spindly fingers as if it were a kitten.

"Just a few more days. That's all I need. They will start to question whether they made the right decision, and without you or this document, they will need a new leader and a new path to follow," the man said, stroking his straight, thin hair. "And voilà! I will appear and save the day!"

Thomas could not hold back his surprise. "Rubbish! You? Lead a nation? Certainly you jest!"

The man leaped across the room in two giant steps, his long, scrawny legs like stilts. He shoved his pointer finger and his monocle just inches from Jefferson's face. "Don't make me angry, sir. You will do what I say, or you will pay. Now, why don't you drink your tea and you will feel better."

The man stood and straightened his double-breasted gray jacket with gold buttons and a black R on the pocket, put his monocle back on his eye, and poured a cup of tea, calming himself.

"Tea? Are you trying to convince me you are civilized? Because you are anything but," Mr. Jefferson spat.

The man put the kettle down. "Just give me a day. I'll bring you to my way of thinking. Just you wait."

Kat's eyes were glued to the date: JULY 2, 1776.

"Now think of everything you know and love about the 4th of July," Liberty said. Kat could feel Liberty standing behind her. Liberty would protect Kat, like Gram always had; Kat could feel it. Kat thought of the parade, the fireworks, the picnic, and all she loved about the celebration in Totsville.

"Now think about everything you know about the history of the 4th of July. Anything will help."

Kat tried to picture men in the white stockings and gold-buttoned jackets, with wigs and funny looking shoes. She pictured them standing around a table with the vital document in front of them. Kat saw a golden pen, and imagined each of them dipping it in ink and signing their names, like Miss Libby described in her history class.

"Good. Good, Kat. Now close your eyes and reach out your hand," Liberty said, calmly and carefully, as if she were a doctor performing a surgery or a burglar trying not to set off an alarm. "Imagine."

Kat reached out and leaned forward, trusting Liberty's voice. Her hands felt the non-slimy mass of Jell-O-like goo first. Then her arms went through, and then—

WHOOSH!

Kat was pulled through in a flash, the same way she went through the doorknob to Libertyland, but this time she didn't stop.

"WEEEEEEE! WOWWWWWW! HEYHEYHEYHIHI-HIHIHOHOHOHO!"

Kat couldn't stop screaming. This was faster and more fun than any water slide at Aqua Thrillway, but if felt sorta like the same thing. She wasn't getting wet, but she was spinning and flipping and sliding. All she could see were fireworks, lots and lots of fireworks. It looked like an entire night sky lit with red and green and blue and white and yellow and gold. Kat had never seen so many sparkles and bursts of color and light.

In the distance, she heard Liberty's voice, getting further and further away. "Don't worry, Kat. You can do this! You can save the 4ᵗʰ of July! We believe in you!"

Everything went black.

THUD.

Kat had landed. Where . . . she did not know.

CHAPTER 5

AN ENLIGHTENED JOURNEY

Kat opened her eyes to total darkness. She heard footsteps. She struggled to stand but knocked her head and fell back down. The footsteps stopped momentarily, but Kat heard them again, louder and closer.

A door swung open in front of her and a young boy stood on the other side of it, staring down at her.

"How did you get in there? Have you been there long? Are you spying on me?" The boy sounded annoyed, but his face looked curious.

Kat saw she was in a closet and had hit her head on a shelf. She crawled out from under it and stood up. In the light of day, they both saw she was taller than the boy. *He's probably a year or two younger*, Kat thought, *and a little too skinny for me. He's not ugly, but look at this outfit! He looks like an old man!*

The boy was a miniature version of the men in tights back in Libertyland. He had on stockings with knickers but wore a shorter jacket than the older men, with a white shirt underneath that ruffled at the neck. Instead of a wig, his loosely curly hair was pulled back with a ribbon like Kat's sister Polly liked to wear in the second grade. He stared at her: up and down, up and down.

Kat still wore her hoodie, sneakers, and shorts, and somehow had made it through time with her backpack. *Maybe we should have thought of better time-traveling clothes*, Kat thought. *Now I'm going to stand out as much as Liberty would.* But she had more important things to think about now.

"So did it work? Am I really here?" Kat marveled, staring around the room.

They were in room that was empty, except for a few tables with wooden chairs and a chalkboard at the front. The chalkboard made Kat think it was a classroom, but it didn't look like any of Kat's classrooms at Totsville Elementary, that's for sure. The walls were bare and had ornate moldings along the edges of the high ceiling. There were no lights, no posters describing nouns and verbs and sentence structure. No photographs, world maps, or drawings kids had done in art class adorned bulletin boards. There were not even desks or computers; only one table with a single candle sat at the front near the chalkboard.

The room echoed as Kat stepped across the hardwood floor and walked past the windows with white wooden trim to the front of the room. The chalkboard read "I will not disobey my parents" over and over again.

The boy followed her to the front of the room. "Are you where? At the Philadelphia State House? Yes," he said, matter-of-factly.

Kat turned around to the boy whose pale face looked as if he'd just seen a ghost. She saw the chalk in his hand and turned to the chalkboard.

Before she could say anything, he stomped his foot and crossed his arms. "But the question remains: How did you get in that closet? And how long have you been there? And . . . and . . ." he kept staring at Kat and her clothes. "What is that you are wearing? It's indecent! I can see your legs!"

Kat laughed because she thought he was joking. When the boy didn't crack a smile she quickly stopped and looked at her shorts. She suddenly felt like a fish out of water and blushed.

Kat remembered her manners and held out her hand. "My name is Kat. What's yours?"

The boy stared at her hand as if it belonged to an alien. He had never shaken a girl's hand before; it was not proper. He cleared his throat, looked at Kat, clasped his hands behind his back, and gave a small bow. "My name is John," he said, puffing out his chest to look taller as he rose. "My parents call me Johnny, but I think that sounds like a little child's name, so I prefer John."

Kat shrugged. "Okay. Nice to meet you, John," Kat said, trying to make her voice sound more serious and proper, like his. She looked at the board again. "So what did you do to get in trouble?"

"That is certainly none of your business! Now tell me at once how you got into that closet before I call my father." His voice was stern.

Kat shook her head. "You're not going to believe me if I told you. But do you really need to go and be a tattletale?"

"Tattletale? What do you mean tattletale? Explain at once before I shout!"

Kat squinted at him. "You don't know what a tattletale is? It's when you run and tell your parents about something someone else is doing wrong when really it has nothing to do with you."

John huffed at her and turned away. "Fine then. Explain how you came to be in that closet and I will not be a *tattletale*." He walked away from the chalkboard, turned, and stood facing Kat, waiting.

Kat was amazed at the way he spoke, like an old person in the . . . *Oh right, I AM in the olden days*, she remembered. "How old are you?"

"I'm nine," he sputtered. "Well, I will be. Next week. And you?"

I knew it! I'm older! Kat smiled. "Eleven. Almost twelve. Next month."

John huffed again. He didn't like that she was older than he was. "And explain your clothing and why you were hiding in that closet."

Kat heard a rustle outside and ran to the window. *Holy macaroni!* Kat thought.

People hurried down dirt roads in a flurry of activity. The women wore bustling long, full dresses that looked like they must have petticoats underneath them. Some held parasols and wore ornate hats and others carried baskets and wore aprons and bonnets. The men in stockings and tailcoats wore long wigs pulled back with tight curls on the side of their heads. Many wore triangular hats or led horse-drawn carriages.

There were no cars or horns honking, no skyscrapers or grocery stores. Kat saw only patches of grass, dirt roads, and brick buildings, like someone had just built a set for a movie set in the . . .

WAIT, Kat thought. *This was definitely not in the 21ˢᵗ century anymore, so maybe it did work?!*

"What year is it?" Kat asked the boy.

"Why, 1776, of course. Why would you ask such a question?"

Double wow. This was unbelievable! Kat remembered the urgency of her mission, and decided she'd better come clean and get it all out in the open. She was losing precious time.

Kat took a deep breath and sighed. "Okay. Here we go. I came from the future. And we have a big problem. A horrible man has kidnapped Thomas Jefferson and the Declaration of Independence is missing. If I don't find them and make sure that the Declaration is signed in two days, then it's going to ruin my life! Oh, and the United States will disappear! I may not even have a life! I may never have been born!"

John ran over to her. "First of all, you contend you 'come from the future'? What is the meaning of that? How did you know about Mr. Jefferson? And about the Declaration? I know only because I risked my life to sneak into a supply carriage to come to the city. I then eavesdropped on my father's conversations upstairs once I arrived."

"Is that why you're in trouble?" Kat asked, looking at the chalkboard.

John dropped his chin. "Yes. I was caught and sent down here. I will be taken back to the farm tomorrow. My father says something is gravely wrong but he won't let me help. I have to go back and help my brothers and sisters and my mother on the farm when all of the action is here, in Philadelphia." He kicked the floor.

Kat certainly knew how it felt to be left out, and wanting to help but instead being forced to do something you didn't want to do. "How many brothers and sisters do you have? I have six."

"I have five," John said.

A light bulb went off in Kat's head. She needed help, and John didn't want to leave the city. "I know a way you won't have to go back to the farm."

John looked up and at Kat. "How? And you still haven't explained your presence in the closet!"

"I'll tell you everything. I just need you to do one thing for me first."

John came running back through the door of the room and threw a wad of material at Kat. She unfolded the mess and held a wrinkled dress and apron in front of her.

John said, "You are lucky. The Ross's upholstery business down the road is the best in town. Mrs. Ross is an excellent seamstress and happened to have this. She also mends uniforms for the militia and is a flag-maker. Mrs. Ross has been kind to me in the past when I have been in her husband's store with my father, so didn't ask many questions—"

Wait. Flag-maker. Ross. Kat interrupted him. "Do you mean Betsy Ross? You got this from Betsy Ross?"

"How did you know Mrs. Ross's first name?" John wondered. He saw Kat begin to take off her hoodie and quickly turned around so that his back was facing Kat and covered his eyes with his hand.

Kat watched him and chuckled. She liked how polite John was. He was uptight and proper, but no boy in her class would bow to her to say hello or turn around because she took off her hoodie. It was a nice change from Demetrius Miller throwing spitballs and farting in the middle of language arts.

"Betsy Ross! This is so totally awesome!" Kat exclaimed as she threw the dress on over her clothes, thinking her shorts would fluff out the dress kind of like a petticoat. "This is way better than my shorts." Kat put her hoodie in her backpack and saw a bandana. She tied it around her head like a bonnet.

"Shorts? Is that the garment you don? And Mrs. Ross is a not particularly large woman, so what is awesome about her?" John asked, his back still to Kat. "Are you decent?" he asked politely.

Kat wrinkled her nose, not sure. "Um, yeah, I guess."

"What do you guess?" John turned around and folded his arms. "You have a funny way with words, but I have upheld my end of our bargain. Now you must tell me. Everything."

"You're going to want to sit down," Kat said.

"I prefer to stand. Thank you."

So Kat proceeded to tell John all about the 4th of July Festival in Totsville, losing the election, Gram taking them to the museum and her magic ticket, meeting Liberty and Libertyland, and the wigged men freaking out.

John interrupted Kat there. "Mr. Adams? Do you mean John Adams?"

Kat shrugged. "Umm, sure. Yeah, you're right. Liberty did say John and I remember him from Miss Libby's class too."

"You met my father?" John asked.

"John Adams is your dad? Are you kidding me? Wow! So you're John QUINCY Adams?" Kat remembered that name too, and it was a big one.

John smiled at Kat's instant recognition of his name. "You know my name?"

Kat finally saw a kid inside that tough, uptight exterior. His pursed lips and stiff shoulders finally relaxed. This made Kat feel much better. Then she realized, *He's exactly what I need: a partner in crime, a fellow adventurer—a Robin to my Batman, a Watson to my Sherlock!*

Now Kat needed to convince JQ of that. "Sure I do. Can I call you JQ?" Kat asked.

John looked at Kat, confused. "It's a nickname, like Johnny, but I think it makes you sound more important." Kat said.

JQ's round cheeks blushed. "I . . . I suppose you can. Continue! Continue! This is fascinating!" Kat could tell JQ was genuinely excited, and she appreciated her captive audience.

Kat told JQ about Liberty's looking bell and seeing the horrible things in Rulerworld, and she described the chalkboards of change. Kat walked up to the chalkboard and demonstrated how she concentrated, the board changed, and she was able to stick her hands through the squishy stuff. She turned to face JQ.

"And the next thing I knew, I was in the closet and you were stomping towards me," Kat said.

JQ was quiet for a moment. Kat thought for sure he wasn't going to believe a word of it. But instead of yelling "Hogwash!" JQ simply stood and looked out the window.

"So it does work after all? We gain our independence from Britain? The rebellion turns into a war and we win? We become the United States? Father will be so elated!"

Kat couldn't believe this kid was nine. He sounded like a grownup, but no grownup Kat knew talked like that. He was so formal. "I guess so, yeah. I mean, yes. It works. The United States of America is our country."

JQ turned to face Kat. "Do you realize what this means?"

"Yes! It means we need to get busy! It means we have less than two days to find Rulerwink, figure out where he's hidden Mr. Jefferson and the Declaration, and get them back here so that the Declaration can be signed. It means we have to hurry!"

JQ shook his head, but was smiling. "It means this is my chance! It means I can show my father that my education can be furthered here. It means I can show him I can help with the rebellion and prove I am old enough to accompany him on such trips! It means, Kat McGee, that we do not have a moment to spare!"

Kat jumped toward JQ, excited. "So you'll help me?"

JQ looked Kat up and down again, like he had done when he first saw her. But this time he threw out his hand as she had done to him. "You are bold and borderline inappropriate, but yes, Kat McGee, future girl, Libertyland traveler, whatever or whoever you are. I will help you. We are going to find Rulerwink and save our new nation!"

He already sounds like a future president, Kat thought and smiled. His enthusiasm almost made Kat forget that they had no leads, no way to figure out where Rulerwink was, and less than two days to make everything happen.

Kat thrust her hand into JQ's outstretched palm and they shook firmly. They had made a pact—an adventure pact. And this adventure could prove to be the most important Kat had ever taken. Gram sent Kat here for a reason, and now she was going to prove that Gram knew what she was doing.

CHAPTER 6

CONTINENTAL WHAT?

The sun set, and JQ lit several candles. He handed one to Kat.

Oh my. I forgot, Kat thought. *No electricity in 1776. Jeepers, this isn't going to be easy.*

JQ said his dad would return at sunrise to fetch him and send him back to the farm. The men in the meeting hall would be working through the night, and JQ had been ordered to go to the boarding house next door to sleep until his father retrieved him. Mrs. Pennypocket, the mistress of the boarding house, was expecting him any minute.

"What's a boarding house? Is it like a hotel?" Kat asked.

JQ furrowed his brow, confused. "A hotel? I don't know what that is. But a boarding house is an establishment where you can rent a room for a night or a week. My father stays when he comes to town."

Kat nodded. "So yeah, it's like a hotel."

JQ shrugged. "We'll need to find a way to get you in without Mrs. Pennypocket seeing you," JQ said. "Luckily she is elderly and can not hear well. Once you are in, we'll need to make an escape plan."

Kat liked the sound of that—like she was James Bond or something.

Getting past Mrs. Pennypocket was like her second grade math class: easy peasy. Mrs. Pennypocket barely looked up from her needlepoint when JQ greeted and talked to her while Kat hid behind a banister in the foyer. The second she saw JQ's hand signal from behind his back, she tiptoed as quickly as she could up the stairs to room number three, trying not to make a sound. Two seconds later, she was behind the door.

JQ came in a few minutes later, laughing. "We should not have fretted so. She's completely unaware!"

"Let's hope getting the Declaration and Thomas Jefferson back are that simple. We'd better get to work."

The two planned and plotted into the night. JQ drew sketches of the State House, and they talked about what they needed to do to get more information. Luckily, the Pennsylvania State House had a lot of nooks and crannies, hidden stairwells, and hiding places, so JQ diligently went over all their options on where and how they could start their mission.

JQ explained to Kat that all the important meetings about the rebellion and their fight for independence from Great Britain took place in the State House. He had begged his father to bring him when he came into the city, but his father always said he was too young or not ready or needed to care for his mother and siblings.

Seeing the look of disappointment on JQ's face, Kat was curious. She asked, "Why do you care about all this stuff anyway? I mean, war and independence and all that? What's the big deal?"

JQ stopped drawing on his map and looked at Kat incredulously. "Surely you do not know what you say!" He raised his voice but quickly quieted again to not arouse suspicion, since he was supposed to be alone and sleeping.

JQ continued. "The Continental Congress is a gathering of the most influential people at the most important time in our history! They are going to decide our fate—whether we will be under British rule or be our own nation. It is such a crucial time. I am too young to fight, but not too young to help."

Kat could tell JQ had a hard time keeping his voice at a whisper. He was practically spitting the words out.

"The Continental what?" Kat asked. *This is why I'm so bad at history and social studies*, Kat thought.

JQ shook his head. "I am shocked that you do not know. Each of the colonies has representatives that form the congress of delegates. They're our governing body."

Kat kind of remembered this part, but JQ was unstoppable. "The congress decided the colonies should be able to rule themselves instead of being governed by the king of England—that we should be able to vote."

Remembering her horrible loss to Roman Rule, Kat huffed, "Voting is overrated. I think whoever really wants it should be able to do it. Sometimes voting isn't fair."

"You would rather have one person tell you what to do and what to say and what to wear? Like this Rulerwink character?"

Kat wavered, but didn't want to admit that to JQ. "I'm just saying that sometimes people know if they would be good leaders. They should be able to try to prove it."

JQ shook his head. "My father says that we should be able to choose a government for ourselves—that we should be a republic of laws, not men. And I agree with him."

That made sense to Kat. She saw how smart JQ was, and she knew he had a point. "I see what you're saying. I just . . . I don't know," Kat said, yawning. She realized then how tired she was.

The two new friends' eyes became heavy and droopy. JQ was fairly certain his father wouldn't return until morning, but in case he checked on JQ in the middle of the night, Kat grabbed a blanket and made a pallet on the floor on the far side of the bed, hidden from sight. They had too much work to do for Kat to be caught.

Kat was still nervous and excited, but traveling through time takes a lot out of a girl. Before she could finish her goodnight prayer, she zonked out.

Kat opened her eyes to JQ prodding her shoulder. "We have to hurry. Wake up!"

Kat blinked a few times. She expected to see her cats Salt and Pepper, but JQ's ponytail and tights reminded her she was far, far away from Totsville and the 21st century. But she felt as if she were at Camp Cibolo: ready to start the day and see what adventure it held. She only had one more day until the course of history would be changed forever, so Kat had to make this one count.

JQ was more than ready. "I'll race you to the State House!"

Before she could argue, he took off.

Kat met JQ by the back basement door where they planned to sneak into the State House. Then, they would find the meeting room where JQ's dad and the other men were discussing the disappearance to see if they could get any clues.

Kat, with her two left feet, clumsily tripped on a floorboard, bumped into a wall, and knocked her head on a ledge in the hallway.

"Ouch!" Kat said, too loudly.

They scanned the hallway; luckily, no one had heard them. JQ, more silent and sneakier than Kat, went a few steps further and pointed to a door in front of them.

Kat and JQ had arrived at the meeting room. JQ assured Kat it wasn't the door the men would come in and out of, but that it would be the best place to overhear any important information. They crouched down and put their ears to the door.

"I can't hear a thing," Kat whispered.

JQ peeked through the keyhole, and Kat tried to squint through the crack in the door. She could make out only two men, both with their colonial wigs and tights, but it sounded like there were a lot more. One looked a lot like the man from Libertyland.

"Is that your dad in the dark blue jacket?" Kat asked.

"Indeed."

They both jumped as Mr. Adams pounded his fists on the table. Now Kat and JQ could hear everything.

"I beg you sir to reconsider!" Mr. Adams said.

"There is no way we will find him in time. The vote is tomorrow," another responded. Kat couldn't be sure, but he looked a lot like Benjamin Franklin.

Kat had seen Benjamin Franklin's face on the one-hundred dollar bill only twice: once, when her parents opened a savings account for her on her tenth birthday and she deposited a bill with Miss Kiana at the bank, and the other time at the Totsville Farm and Fresh grocery store when Mrs. Kemp paid for her groceries with one.

But Kat couldn't forget that face! Mr. Franklin looked younger, but Kat was sure it was the famous inventor. *Wow! The guy who flew his kite and discovered electricity is on the other side of this door,* Kat thought.

"I think we need to send out a band of soldiers from here to Boston!" another man shouted. Then came a lot of shouting and finger pointing.

"That is not the most prudent course of action, sir. We should wait until we hear something from the kidnapper."

"First and foremost, we need to decipher this message!"

"We are wasting valuable time!"

The men took turns looking at an unrolled scroll of paper on the table. They screamed at each other. No one agreed on anything.

"They're never going to find the culprit if they keep arguing like that," JQ said.

Kat was again impressed with JQ's maturity. He was right. "I know. It sounds like one of our POFF meetings." JQ looked at her quizzically. "I'll explain later."

On the table was the clue the stealthy pair needed. Kat and JQ must get their hands on the scroll.

"We need that scroll. If we can decipher the message they keep talking about," Kat suggested, "then we're in business."

JQ considered this. "I don't know how we will get into that room undetected."

Kat was great at creating distractions. "Leave it to me. You'll know when to run in. But you'll have to be fast."

"Like the wind," JQ replied.

Kat slipped and scooted her way back down the stairs and hallways to the front door. She went out into the street, and was careful no one saw her as she headed around the building. She could see the figures of the men through the window and surveyed the area for her options. A smile spread across Kat's face; she knew exactly what to do.

Kat sprinted over to a horse that was tied up a few feet away and jumped on it. She may not have won any ribbons in the horse show, but Camp Cibolo, not to mention her time with the reindeer at the School of Christmas Spirit, did teach her a thing or two.

Kat soothed and talked to the horse then climbed up and led it to the nearest window. The horse didn't seem to notice anything out of the ordinary and readily followed her lead. She carefully slipped off the saddle and opened the window nearest a table in the far corner of the room. It held two teapots, bunches of cups, spoons, and sugar cubes.

Kat now saw the room more fully. It was very similar to the one where she met JQ except much larger. Instead of benches there were several tables with two candlesticks on each and green tablecloths. Each had two wooden chairs, all facing the front of the room, where the men now surrounded the larger table. With all the shouting, the men didn't hear Kat at all.

Kat opened her backpack and pulled out the apple she had shoved in before the road trip to Philadelphia. With so many kids, Kat knew Gram's snack packs wouldn't last long, so she made sure she had her own provisions. Kat let the horse take one bite of the apple, and then set it on the table directly next to the sugar cubes. If there was anything horses liked more than apples, it was sugar cubes.

Kat climbed back down from the window and gave the horse a big slap on his rear end.

"NEAHHHHH!" the horse bellowed, as he shoved his head through the window and started chomping on the sugar, knocking over plenty of tea cups in the process.

Everyone in the room turned toward the ruckus in the corner. They rushed over to see how the horse could have put his head through the window as JQ slid silently through the door on the other side of the room. He grabbed the scroll off the front table where the men had just stood. Across the room, the men studied the empty sugar dish while the horse tried to pick up the apple core. JQ carefully tiptoed back out the door.

As he closed the door, he heard someone say, "What on earth do we have here?"

Kat met JQ in front of the State House.

"Nice distraction, miss," JQ said as he bowed. It was his turn to be impressed with Kat. "You may be forward, but you have a daring spirit."

"Why thank you, sir," she said with a curtsy. She felt as if she were rehearsing a play in Mrs. Borden's drama class. "Now, let's see if it was worth it."

The cabin was littered with flyers, maps, banners, and carvings: RULERWORLD, *Romulus Rulerwink will save the colonies!*, Rulerworld Plaza, The Rules of Romulus Rulerwink. An entire table was covered in Rulerworld paraphernalia, and next to it were bags of tea and a kettle. Other than that, the cabin was empty.

Thomas was distraught. The crazy bug-eyed man was going to ruin everything! He stared at him but felt helpless. He was still tied to the chair. Rulerwink gathered all of his things, even the tea. He was preparing to leave. He lifted the Declaration and rolled it up.

"Don't take the Declaration!" Thomas shouted.

Rulerwink scoffed. "You do not want to be parted with your precious document. Isn't that sentimental?"

"What are you going to do with me? What are you going to do with it?"

"So inquisitive? Well, Mr. Jefferson, if you must know. I'm going to use your own document against you. I will ride back into the city tonight, and tomorrow, without your dutiful presence, I will present the congress with a new plan—mine. And I will persuade them it is the better one, I can assure you."

"I believe you underestimate the will of the men of the congress," Thomas replied.

"Do not doubt I will have a very *persuasive* argument."

Thomas did not like the sound of that. He tried to stall. "And you're going to leave me here? Alone? What if someone finds me?"

"Out here? Ha!" Rulerwink huffed. "Ah, no. Those thinkers can't agree on anything! They will be arguing and trying to decipher my message all night long. Once I arrive with pertinent information about the disappearance of dear Mr. Jefferson, I will have their attention. That is all I need."

"What if I escape?" Thomas proposed. "I will have you arrested immediately upon your arrival!"

Rulerwink laughed. "Escape? Tom! Come, come. Now who is underestimating whom? I assure you, it will not be possible."

Mr. Jefferson didn't like the sound of that either.

Kat and JQ hurried down the road to a nearby park and hid behind a bush so they wouldn't be seen. It was hot and they sat in the shade, out of sight. The note was on a scroll; they unrolled it and read:

> *Until you see that I should lead you,*
> *I will take the man and his words too.*
> *You think freedom begins with him and his doc,*
> *But only a Ruler can be your rock.*
> *Can you find him? Do you need a sign?*
> *A far away place where the stars don't shine . . .*

Kat read it five times. She had no clue what it meant. But JQ squinted his eyes on the last phrase and read it aloud over and over again.

Kat asked, "Far away place? Like another state? What if Rulerwink took Jefferson to Virginia? Or Massachusetts?"

JQ shook his head. "They would not have had time to go far. It's been only a day since Jefferson's been missing." JQ turned and looked toward the State House.

Kat said, "Where the stars don't shine? Underground? A cave?"

JQ shrugged. "I don't know of any nearby caves, and underground would be too risky. We need to find more clues."

"But we don't have time for clues! We need to get going," Kat argued.

"Stars don't shine . . . stars don't shine," JQ repeated. "Well, all we can do is keep looking. Maybe it will come to us. Let's go, Miss McGee."

"But where are we going? We don't have any idea where he is," Kat said, frustrated.

JQ held out his hand to help Kat stand and explained, "We need someone to help us cover more ground. Two children asking a lot of questions are going to look suspicious. I think I know someone who will help us, and maybe by the time we find him we'll know where to go."

Kat followed, but grabbed JQ's arm to stop him. "Your father is going to realize you're missing any second, and that's going to put everyone on alert. Not to mention the fact we took the scroll, their only lead."

JQ smiled. "Don't worry. The person we seek is fast. We just have to find him."

"Who?" Kat asked.

"A friend of my family. He has a horse and if we can get to him, I know he would help. Now, try to blend in and don't look so . . . so . . . futuristic."

Kat rolled her eyes. "That's funny. Where do we have to look? Where does he live?"

"Patience, future girl," JQ said.

"Just tell me his name, at least!"

JQ stopped in the middle of the road, turned, and looked at Kat. "Ever heard of a man named Paul Revere?"

CHAPTER 7

THE SECOND MIDNIGHT RIDE OF PAUL REVERE

Finding Paul Revere proved difficult—especially when Kat wanted to look and stop and talk about all the things she saw, or more noticeably, what she *didn't* see. JQ didn't know about cars or stop lights or paved streets; horses and carriages were the only way to get around town besides your own two feet. This place was more rustic than Camp Cibolo.

No one was talking on phones or texting or playing computer games—people were actually talking to each other, greeting Kat and JQ as they walked down the dirt street. Kat looked in windows and saw kids playing with wooden toys and dolls that looked like they were made from socks and straw. Uniformed men with drums over their shoulders walked the streets in lines, marching and drumming.

These people didn't know the wonders of air conditioning and couldn't keep food cool in refrigerators. Even in the heat there was no sunscreen to slather on or sprinklers to run through; no bathing suits or swimming pools, no water slides or theme parks. Kat insisted that summer in 1776 must be boring.

JQ got defensive. "It's not boring! We have plenty of fun things to do!"

"Name two," Kat teased. JQ mumbled something about the silly future, and Kat giggled.

Kat and JQ had gone to every mill and blacksmith shop in town. No one had seen Paul Revere. Kat was starting to get hungry. Since she had sacrificed her apple to create their major distraction, she had no snacks left.

"Are you hungry?" Kat asked JQ. "Guess you don't have a drive thru or a supermarket in 1776." Kat laughed, even though JQ clearly didn't get the joke.

"We have a general store, but I have no coins or commodity money," JQ said, rubbing his belly. "But I am famished. Maybe Mr. Revere will have something at the mill . . . if we ever find the mill where he's working, that is."

Kat didn't have any money either, but she was guessing her allowance wouldn't be acceptable in 1776 anyway.

JQ looked worried. "Not only can we not find Paul Revere, we still haven't figured out where Rulerwink is hiding Mr. Jefferson. Poor Mr. Jefferson. I hope he's unharmed—if he's even still alive!"

Kat stopped. That's it! Kat knew he was still alive because she *saw* him. She saw Mr. Jefferson in Liberty's looking bell!

"I've seen where he is. Well, not where he is, but I saw he was tied to a chair in a cabin." Kat had mentioned Liberty's bell briefly in telling her story but had skipped the details.

"Tell me everything! What do you remember?"

Kat closed her eyes. It had happened so fast. "A log cabin. It was dark. I think an hourglass and a candle were on a table."

"That doesn't narrow it down," JQ said. "What else? Anything!?"

"Umm . . . oh, there was a tattered flag. And a carving in the wall I think? It looked kind of like a star?"

"Hmm . . . tattered flag. . . star in the wall," JQ thought about this.

"*A far away away place where the stars don't shine!* That's what he's talking about! The star on the wall! A carving doesn't shine."

JQ jumped up and down. "I've got it! I've got it! Of course! He's talking about the Freedom Fort! It's a secluded cabin where the star and flag were hung to symbolize freedom for the colonies. Some generals have used it as a safe place during the rebellion.

I have only seen it once, but it's hidden along the Wissahickon Creek in the forest far outside of town. The trees are so dense around the cabin that one can barely see the night sky. That's why it's been such a good hiding place."

"Freedom Fort? Well, I guess no one would think to go there to hold someone else hostage. Sort of against the point."

"Exactly! He's being ironic. Rulerwink is clever."

"Clever and evil," Kat remarked. She looked around. "Let's get going! Is it too far to walk? Or ride? Now we really need to find Paul Revere!"

The newly energized duo continued far beyond the city center. The sun was getting lower in the sky, and Kat tried to hide her anxiety. If they didn't find him before nightfall, only one day remained. What if they found nothing at the Freedom Fort? They would have wasted all this precious time, and she would fail!

Fields and trees surrounded them, and they heard a few shots and rumbles in the distance.

Kat had to admit she was getting nervous. "Should we be trying to hide? There is a war going on, right?"

"It's not a full-scale war yet, and most of the battles are no-where near here," JQ said, trying to mask his own fear as well. "I saw a horrible battle near my family's farm. Gruesome. But I'm confident what we hear now is the militia practicing." They continued in silence as the sun set.

"I know Mr. Revere is here only for a short time, so I hope we don't miss him. We'd never make it to Boston, and I believe Mr. Revere is the only adult who would help."

"Why would he not tell your father? Are you sure we can trust him?"

"Mr. Revere believes everyone can help the cause in his or her own way, unlike my father, who wants me back on the farm with my mother. And Mr. Revere has shown it. He's been a courier, an infantryman, and a silversmith, and was recently promoted to lieutenant colonel! I think he will feel it his duty to help us. And his midnight ride was built on secrecy. He's good with secrets."

As darkness descended a light flickered in the distance. Kat thought the shadow ahead looked like a barn more than a mill, but she honestly didn't know the difference. "Maybe we can stop there," Kat sighed. She needed to rest. They had been walking for hours.

"Our last hope. Mr. Revere is here, or we've missed him and will have to devise a new plan." JQ perked up. "I'll race you there!"

JQ loved to race. Kat ran to keep up.

They arrived at the door to the mill and heard a voice. JQ knocked softly, and the voice stopped.

"Who is there?" a voice questioned from behind the door.

JQ cleared his throat. "I am looking for Mr. Paul Revere."

Silence.

Kat and JQ waited.

And waited.

Finally the door opened two inches, and Kat saw a single eye peek from within. A low, raspy voice prodded, "Who wants to know?"

Kat piped up, knowing they probably had one shot at keeping his attention. "Tell him we have important information about the Declaration of Independence."

The door swung open quickly and before Kat and JQ could see or say anything more, they were pulled inside.

A short, older man with a square face and round, red cheeks looked at them. He wore a long-sleeved shirt with puffy sleeves and a green vest over it, along with knickers that were maybe a little too tight. His brown hair was pulled back in a ponytail, and his hands and face were covered in black smudges as if he'd been sweeping chimneys. He held a lamp to their faces.

"Why, you are children! What on earth brings you out here at night? Where are your parents? And why do you speak of the Declaration so flippantly?"

Kat and JQ looked at each other and swallowed. JQ nodded to Kat.

"Because someone has stolen it and we think we know where it is," she sputtered.

JQ picked up where Kat left off. "And we need your help to get there. Quickly. Time is not on our side."

The man looked at JQ. "How do you know who I am? And how did you find me?"

"You know my father, Mr. Revere," JQ said, dropping his chin. "John Adams."

Paul Revere thrust the lamp in JQ's face. His voice changed and face softened. He smiled. "Young Johnny? Is that you? Well now I hardly recognized you; you're quite a dapper young man. Does your father know you're here? He would have a fit!"

"He would, sir, and no, he doesn't know. Please do not send word. We truly do have important, sensitive information, Mr. Revere. We ask for your secrecy," JQ begged.

Paul looked at them both and took a deep breath. Without saying another word, he turned and shuffled into the darkened room. Kat and JQ glanced at each other and followed the light of Paul Revere's lamp.

Paul led the duo into a room filled with barrels and barrels of gunpowder. *Maybe that's why his face looks like it's covered in charcoal!* Kat thought. Mr. Revere excused his mess and appearance. He explained he was set to open a gunpowder mill in Boston so was in Philadelphia to learn the process.

He motioned for JQ and Kat to sit on a nearby bench and sat down in a large leather chair at a desk.

Paul Revere leaned forward and said, "Well? I'm intrigued. Do tell how you came to be here. Would you like a cup of tea to warm your little bodies? It is no trouble."

Kat and JQ shook their heads. *Everyone and their tea!* Kat thought.

They took turns telling their story: Kat traveling through the chalkboard and landing in the closet at the State House, JQ grabbing the scroll while Kat distracted the men in the congress, figuring out the message, and finally about Liberty's looking bell and Rulerwink's plan to take over the entire country and make it Rulerworld.

"What a tale!" Paul exclaimed.

Kat hung her head. "You don't believe us, do you?"

"Let me see this message of which you speak."

Kat grabbed the scroll out of her backpack, handed it to Paul, and as he read his brow furrowed.

Paul straightened his vest and rose from his chair. "On the contrary, young lady. I have no choice but to believe you. The freedom of our country is at stake."

Kat and JQ stood, amazed.

"So you will take us to the Freedom Fort? Tonight?" JQ asked expectantly.

"You certainly can not go alone. It must be tonight because I am back to Boston tomorrow!"

"But it's hours away," JQ said. "We won't get there until after midnight!"

Kat couldn't believe how late it was. The day had flown by.

Paul Revere smiled. "That's my favorite time to ride."

After grabbing a small loaf of bread for the two wary travelers, Paul saddled up his mare, Delilah, and pulled Kat up in front, on her neck. JQ jumped on behind Paul.

"Young adventurers, let us be off to the Freedom Fort! Hold on to your hats!" Paul announced into the night. JQ gave a love pat to Delilah's backside, and they were off into the night.

★ ★ ★

Although it wasn't quite as exhilarating as riding in Santa's sleigh with Rudolph at the helm, Kat had to admit that there was something about galloping through the darkened forests of Pennsylvania with the real, live Paul Revere that made her stomach do a few back flips of joy. She felt safe with Paul and JQ, even though she knew that, in this time and this place, she was probably anything but secure.

They had been riding for hours, and Kat must have dozed off. She awoke when Paul pulled on the reins and Delilah slowed to a walk. Kat saw a clearing in the forest ahead and hoped they were close. Beside them a small river slowly crawled along, its water low in the middle of summer.

"We should be quiet from here on. The Freedom Fort is just ahead," Paul whispered.

Kat noticed a small flickering light, but it quickly disappeared. Delilah went a few more steps, and Kat saw the shadow of a cabin. The horse stopped.

They waited. And watched. And listened.

There was no sound or movement coming from inside, and at first it looked like it was empty. Maybe JQ had been wrong about the star and Jefferson and the Declaration weren't here at all. Kat hoped they had not come all this way for nothing.

Suddenly a BOOM came out of the darkness; something had fallen and crashed to a wooden floor. Another flicker of light, and Kat could see the window of the cabin more clearly. Someone was inside.

Paul whispered, "You two stay here. I will see who, or what, is inside."

"No!" Kat gasped. "I mean, no, sir. We made it this far, we want to go." JQ was impressed with Kat's courage.

"You must stay behind me," Paul insisted.

Kat and JQ promised to remain behind him.

The three slowly, carefully made their way to the porch of the cabin, leaves crunching beneath their feet. A creaky first step caused Paul to stop and pause, and he climbed three more before crouching next to the window by the front door. JQ and Kat closely followed and did the same.

The three pulled their heads up and peeked in the window of the cabin.

A man was tied to a chair, but he had fallen over and was on his side on the floor. A nub of a candle on a small table was flickering.

No one else was in the one-room cabin.

"That's got to be him! This looks like the cabin in Liberty's bell," Kat said.

"We will soon see, young lady," Paul said.

Kat appreciated his chutzpah.

Mr. Revere stood and crept to the doorway. He pulled a weird instrument out of his vest and held it close to his chest.

"One . . . two . . . THREE!" Paul yelled as he pushed the door open and threw his hand out as if he had a sword, except the instrument was instead the size of an oversized toothbrush.

"Don't shoot! I have been kidnapped! Please help me!" the tied-up man shouted from the floor.

Kat and JQ ran to Paul's side and looked at the fallen man.

Paul took one look in the dim moonlight streaming from the window and said, "Well, hello, Mr. Jefferson. Although I hate to find you in this state, it is a pleasure to finally meet you. I'm Paul Revere." He pointed to Kat and JQ. "And these children helped me find you."

Mr. Jefferson looked at the three of them, astonished.

"What is that?" JQ asked Paul, pointing to the small sharp instrument.

"Oh, this little thing. I spent some time as a dentist. It looks more dangerous than it is."

Kat wasn't interested in Mr. Revere's repurposed dental tool. She couldn't stop staring at the man on the floor. She wanted to capture this moment because Anjali wouldn't believe her in a million years.

If someone had told Kat that she would be standing here, on the dusty floor of a cabin in the middle of a Pennsylvania forest in 1776, staring at the author of the Declaration of Independence and the future president of the United States, she would have laughed until she cried. Now she wished she had asked for an iPhone for Christmas.

After untying Mr. Jefferson and relighting the lamps, the rescuers got quite an earful from him. They didn't have a chance to explain how they had found him, and at that moment, he didn't seem to care.

"We do not have a second to spare. This traitorous man Romulus Rulerwink is threatening everything for which we have laboriously toiled. He took the Declaration with him, and I'm afraid he has some evil plans for the future of our budding country."

Kat only understood about half of what he said, but she couldn't help but interject, "I know. I've seen the awful place. It's *so* not fun."

Thomas eyed Kat with a curious stare, wondering who this strange looking girl with a bright pack on her back was. "I . . . yes, I agree. How do you know that, young one?"

Kat opened her mouth but the only thing that came out was her name. "I'm Kat. Kat McGee. I like your shoes." *Shoes? Was the first thing I said to the future president of the United States about shoes?* Kat was mortified.

The child perplexed Mr. Jefferson. He knew not of her reference to his shoes, but he turned his attention back to Paul and the problem at hand. "Rulerwink is headed to the State House now to be present when the congress convenes at dawn. We must stop or intercept him. Mr. Revere! We must go, now!"

"I'm sorry, sir, but there are now four of us. And one horse. What do you propose we do?"

Mr. Jefferson scratched his chin. "A predicament indeed."

"Who is this man? Why does he want to do such harm?" JQ said, inspecting the cabin for clues. A few Rulerwink flyers and a couple tea bags were the only things left strewn about. "There is a missing piece of this puzzle, but if we are to stop him we need to go. Now."

The four of them stood in the center of the cabin, thinking. *Psychedelic Sally would come in handy right now*, Kat thought. As the group contemplated a plan, a breeze sweeping through the window blew out one of the lamps.

"Please, sir, if you will relight the torch . . . " Mr. Jefferson said to Paul. "Rather, the lamp. My mind is elsewhere."

That's it! Kat realized. *Liberty's torch!*

"I've got it! I've got it! I know how we can get back in time!" Kat shouted, jumping up and down. "Well, not *back in time* to another year, but back to the State House before Rulerwink."

The three looked at Kat with disbelief and doubt.

But, as Kat pulled the pencil-sized contraption out of her backpack, and the glowing torch expanded and grew right before their eyes, their disbelief became awe.

"WHAT IS THAT?" JQ asked, his eyes as big as saucers.

Kat's face beamed as brightly as the torch she held. "Liberty's torch. To light our way."

CHAPTER 8

A SPELL AT
THE STATE HOUSE

Romulus Rulerwink's plan was working even better than he had imagined. With Thomas Jefferson tucked far away and the Declaration of Independence and the Rulerworld Rulebook under each arm, he had no doubt these poor excuses for leaders would see his vision for the future was infinitely better. Soon, his long-envisioned plans of Rulerworld would finally become a reality.

Romulus walked up the steps of the State House just as the sun was rising. He knew the disappearance of Jefferson and the Declaration had put the members into a frantic frenzy; he would be the calming voice. They would be gathered, tired from a long night of trying unsuccessfully to settle on a course of action. And he had a secret weapon. It was the perfect moment to pounce.

Kat didn't know exactly how to work Liberty's torch. Was she supposed to simply point it in the direction they wanted to go? Or was she supposed to order it to lead them back to the city. Kat remembered what Liberty said when she gave her the torch: *It will show you the path if lost, shine the light if darkness overcomes,*

make the impossible seem possible, and point the way home when you're ready.

JQ climbed on the horse with Paul, and Kat instinctively grabbed Mr. Jefferson's hand, either out of fear or to make sure she wouldn't be alone if something weird happened. Jefferson was startled by the gesture, but he gently squeezed her hand, and Kat immediately felt better.

Kat pointed the torch in the direction they were to go.

Silence. Stillness.

Uh oh, Kat thought. *What if I've broken Liberty's torch!*

Kat tried to keep her voice steady. "Uh . . . maybe it just needs to get warmed up," she suggested. She shook it and looked to see if the torch had a switch. Nothing.

Kat tried again. But as she pointed the torch, Kat concentrated fully on the task at hand, like she did with Liberty and the chalkboard to 1776.

Kat closed her eyes, and she slowly felt a prickling feeling in her feet, like the pins and needles when her feet fell asleep. The tingling moved up her body, and she opened her eyes and looked at the others.

Kat saw a dim light encircle the group, as if a giant bubble was being blown around them. And like her first feeling in Libertyland, a force of energy lifted the bubble off the ground and started to gently, slowly move them forward. Even Delilah the horse, carrying Paul and JQ, was strangely being pulled up off the ground into the darkness with Kat and Mr. Jefferson.

"Egads!" Paul Revere proclaimed. "I can hardly believe my eyes, but it appears we are moving southward!"

JQ's mouth was open, but he was in such shock he couldn't speak. The bubble started to gain speed, and soon the trees and bushes were flying by them. They were not far from the ground; it felt as if they were cruising on a gentle but speedy moving sidewalk.

As Kat continued to point the torch wherever Mr. Jefferson directed her, she put her other hand into the glowing film that encircled them.

Boing! It bounced right back.

"It looks like the sun is about to come up," Kat said. "We will never make it in time. What are we going to do?!"

"Do not ask, little lassie. ACT! Action is what defines us. You must believe in yourself and your actions so others will believe in you as well."

"Here, here!" Paul and JQ said in unison.

"We must persevere, but remain calm. Nothing gives one person so much advantage over another as to remain always cool and unruffled under all circumstances," Mr. Jefferson encouraged.

Kat took a deep breath and let it go, trying to calm herself. She got such a kick out of how they all talked. She liked it. And every word Mr. Jefferson said was thoughtful and wise. *No wonder he became president*, Kat thought and smiled.

They reached the outskirts of town as the sun peeked over the horizon. The landscape around them was no longer a blur; they were slowing down. And just as they came to Main Street, Kat felt her feet touch the ground. Delilah started trotting forward, and the bubble of light and speed disintegrated.

Kat shook the torch. Maybe the spell was broken because the torch started to shrink in her hand. "Wonder if this thing takes batteries," Kat joked.

JQ looked at her, perplexed. "Batteries? A battery of what?"

The three of them looked at Kat. She'd have to explain that later, too.

"It's the 4ᵗʰ of July," Kat said, worry in her voice she tried to hide.

"'tis indeed. Today is the day we will alter the course of history," Mr. Jefferson said.

Kat looked at him. "Either you will, or Rulerwink will do it for you. But I'm ready."

JQ shouted, "I am with you Kat McGee."

"Then let us run to the State House and save our independence!" Kat proclaimed.

Thomas Jefferson and Paul Revere smiled proudly at the young freedom fighters.

"One man, or woman, in this case, with courage is a majority," Jefferson said, winking at Paul Revere. "Beware, Romulus Rulerwink. You face a fierce foe."

For the first time in weeks, the meeting room was quiet. The 55 men of the Continental Congress sat in chairs at the small tables in the meeting room, drinking tea and staring intently at the speaker at the front of the room. Romulus Rulerwink mesmerized them.

Rulerwink had waited for this moment his entire life. He had a captive audience; he could make them listen.

"We need a world with order, and I can give it to you. We need a nation of safety, and I can give it to you. You don't need Jefferson and you don't need this," Romulus said, pulling out the Declaration of Independence.

A collective gasp rang through the meeting room.

"I have convinced Mr. Jefferson that my way is the right way, and he willingly gave me his document and told me to do whatever necessary to change it."

The men were in a trance. Their eyes were glazed as they sat watching him. Rulerwink had all the answers.

Romulus continued, "I will take responsibility so you don't have to worry about anything. I have already convinced Great Britain that this is the way of the future. They have agreed to stop the war and to release the colonies to me."

Sighs and "ahhhs" spread across the room.

"The laws will be simple. No one will be hurt or fearful of their future again."

The room was silent.

"My name is Romulus Rulerwink, and together, we will create Rulerworld!"

The door slammed open and the fantastic four stood facing the room: Kat, JQ, Paul Revere, and Thomas Jefferson.

"Not if we have anything to do with it," Kat announced. "First you'll have to get past us."

★ ★ ★

Kat sounded a lot more confident than she felt. They had no plan beyond storming the meeting room. They hadn't had time to plot how to confront or capture Rulerwink. But she was glad to see that Rulerwink was completely thrown off guard.

"Fraud!" Mr. Jefferson shouted.

Although everyone in the room was turned toward the four intruders, Kat found it strange that not one man was on his feet. Gone were the shouting matches she had witnessed from the window. No one was arguing. No one was even talking.

Could it be that Romulus had truly convinced them that Rulerworld was better than the United States? They looked as if they had fallen under a Rulerwink spell!

Mr. Jefferson and Paul Revere were equally as surprised at the reaction of the congress, or lack thereof.

After his initial shock at seeing the four of them standing in the meeting room, Rulerwink regained his composure, straightened his monocle, and spread his long, skinny arms wide. An evil smile spread across his face. "Welcome. Welcome to our brave new world. I'm afraid if you are looking for this," Romulus said, reaching for and lifting the Declaration, "you are just a tad too late."

Rulerwink raised the Declaration of Independence and put a candle beneath it. In seconds, it was up in flames.

Kat gasped, putting her hand over her mouth to stop a scream.

JQ cried out, "Nooo!"

Paul Revere held the feisty boy from charging toward the gaunt young man, whose skeletal appearance made him look much older—and more threatening.

Mr. Jefferson stood still, dropping his chin to his chest, defeated.

"But I consider myself a fair man," Rulerwink said. "Why don't we have a vote? You people love your votes, do you not?"

Kat looked all around the room. Something was fishy. The men looked at Romulus unblinking and silent. What was wrong with them? Where was the fight?

Romulus raised his hand. "All those in favor of the rules of Rulerworld, the world free from responsibility, but full of safety and order, raise your hands and say 'aye.'"

The hands started going up, one by one, and echoes of "aye" spread across the room.

Kat felt uneasy. Something wasn't right. Rulerwink had done something to these men; she was sure of it.

Even more telling than the ashes of the document at the front of the room was this "vote": the glazed looks of the men in congress, the trance-like motions as they sipped tea and raised their hands . . . the vacant stares were the same as those Kat had seen from the future Rulerworld in Liberty's looking bell. Their faces were spooky—they could have popped out of one of her brother's zombie video games.

Kat swallowed hard and realized her mouth was dry. A drink of water sounded great, and she saw the teakettles on the table.

Wait, Kat thought. *Tea on the table with the sugar cubes . . . tea pots in the cabin . . . everyone drinking tea, almost simultaneously . . . like it was planned . . . that's it!*

"You *do* have them under a spell," Kat said. "You used the tea!"

It was only a guess, but instantly Kat knew she was right.

Rulerwink's smile faded, his already pale face turning a sick shade of gray.

Everything that followed happened very quickly:

Kat ran to the tea table, smelling the tea bags—the florid, sweet smell made her dizzy, and she had not even tasted it!

Revere raced to Rulerwink, who had lunged for the nearest window in an attempt to escape.

Jefferson grabbed a pitcher of water and started throwing it on the men's faces, not knowing what could get them out of this trance but hoping the water would help.

JQ, following Jefferson's lead, tried to shake each man out of his stupor.

Meanwhile, short Mr. Revere had Rulerwink pinned to the wall.

Rulerwink's voice seemed smaller when he started to scream, "You can not stop me! You will not stop Rulerwink! They are mine!"

The spell was wearing off. The men were confused, and they looked around the room as if they were in a foreign world.

Thomas Jefferson walked slowly, deliberately over to Rulerwink, stared him straight in the face and said, "You have an immense amount of explaining to do."

Everyone in the room crowded behind Jefferson and surrounded Rulerwink.

Kat folded her arms in front of her. "Anytime you're ready . . . sir."

CHAPTER 9

LIFE, LIBERTY, AND THE PURSUIT OF ROMULUS

Romulus stood against the wall, as motionless as a deer caught in headlights.

At first, he was combative. "You are making a huge mistake! You don't know what you're doing!"

"It is you who has made a grave mistake," Jefferson uttered.

Rulerwink looked around the room at the group of angry men surrounding him. He looked to the doors and windows to see if there was another way to escape. But Rulerwink soon realized he was outnumbered. He had no chance against more than 50 men.

He sank to the floor, and his long and tall frame seemed to shrivel as the crowd fully woke from their trance and moved toward him, angry and wanting answers. Rulerwink caved, looking more like a frightened child than the vicious tyrant he was trying to be.

Two men ran up and tied Rulerwink's hands behind him. Jefferson motioned for them to step aside. Rulerwink wasn't going anywhere.

The crowd wanted answers.

"Why would you do this?"

"Who are you?"

"Where did you come from?"

"Did you poison us?"

Even Kat stepped forward and shouted, "Why do you hate independence and everything these men have worked so hard for?"

Romulus didn't know where to begin. The room quieted and he finally looked up. "I wanted some recognition. I wanted people to see and understand I have something to give and share," Romulus said, his voice soft and weak.

A man stepped forward. "I recognize you. You used to work with my doctor in Boston."

Romulus nodded. "I am a scientist and alchemist by trade." He looked at Kat and JQ in the middle of the crowd. "You meddling kids. I was once like you. I was a smart and clever child, but no one would listen to me or my ideas. My teachers loved me, but my peers hated me. I wanted only to be *known* for something great."

Kat knew what it felt like to want recognition.

Romulus continued. "I knew I could be better than any president, better than a king. I wanted to be a ruler! I had grand plans for this nation, and all of you ruined them." He looked like he was going to cry. With a deep sigh he added, "And now none of you will know the freedom of Rulerworld."

Jefferson looked at Rulerwink, disappointed. "You are wrong, sir. You do not understand our mission. You do not understand what freedom means."

JQ asked, "How did you put everyone in a trance? Are you some kind of sorcerer?"

Romulus looked ashamed. "I am no magician. But I would go to any length do get what I wanted. I would lie to make people like me; I would cheat to win an election; I would steal to make myself seem more important."

"And people believed you? How did you get this far?" Kat asked.

"I could always pass the blame or convince others I was in the right. And when I couldn't do it on my own, I concocted a way to force people to believe me," Romulus admitted.

Paul Revere interjected, "With the tea."

Romulus nodded. "As an alchemist, the Boston Tea Party gave me the most brilliant idea. I took the opportunity to use the tea, which I knew was readily available in this State House, to force you all to listen to me. A mixture of a few herbs and powders was all it took." Romulus had no fight left in his voice. "Rulerworld would have been the greatest place on earth."

Instead of being afraid of Rulerwink, Kat felt sorry for him. She also began to realize he didn't even know how wrong he was. He truly believed this horrible world he wanted to create would be an improvement.

Kat took a step toward Rulerwink. Mr. Jefferson tried to hold her back, but she stepped away from his protective arm and toward the defeated man crouched in a ball on the floor.

"Don't you see?" Kat said to him. "Rulerworld is the opposite of freedom. You wanted to be in charge of everything and everyone, and have everyone do what you said. But that's not freedom."

JQ joined Kat and said, "Freedom is each person making choices and decisions for himself. Freedom is being a part of a community where people are treated equally and have respect for each other's similarities *and* differences."

Kat looked up and saw John Adams look at his son and her and smile proudly. The men in the circle around them were nodding their heads, agreeing with them.

Jefferson smiled. "The children are correct. And with that freedom comes responsibility, and sometimes you aren't always going to agree with people or want to do what they say."

Mr. Adams added, "And so we all learn to compromise. If we listen and respect the ideas and arguments of others, we can all learn from friends and even foes."

As Mr. Jefferson and Mr. Adams spoke, Kat began to realize something about herself: Not only had Roman Rule been like Rulerwink in his treatment of Kat and other kids in school, Kat had been just as wrong. She didn't want to participate in the POFF because she hadn't won the election; she didn't want to compromise and listen to other people's ideas. She had not been responsible. Kat had been greedy and was as guilty as Roman Rule, maybe even more so.

Kat looked at Rulerwink. "You don't always have to be the leader to be a part of something special. You are smart. You are only responsible for your actions, not everyone else's. You can't control what people do, just how you respond. And when you all work together, that's when great things happen."

Rulerwink sighed. "No one will ever want to work with me now. I am sure to be an outcast the rest of my life. I have done terrible things. I am finished."

Jefferson said, "Not necessarily. It is true you will be tried in a court for your mistakes. You will suffer consequences for your actions this day. But that government is the strongest of which every man feels himself a part."

"Yes, a nation is only as strong as her people," Mr. Adams said. "We want strong and smart men, who with dignity work together for this country we are trying to create. We ask all who are willing to be a part of that vision to join us."

Kat saw that she was not only getting a history lesson right in front of her, it was also all starting to make sense. She understood why Miss Libby tried so hard to teach Kat about all of these men. When they created the United States of America, they had a vision of what the country could become. Kat could see now how important that vision was.

Kat also understood why Gram wanted her to come here. She was trying to teach her a lesson—a life lesson. Kat saw how important it was to be responsible for your actions, and what freedom truly meant.

Romulus sat up and said, "After everything I have done, you would let me join you?"

"If you understand and admit your mistakes, take your punishment, and agree with the Declaration of Independence and all that it stands for, yes, we would gladly have you," Mr. Adams said.

With that, a stricken look fell across Romulus' face: the Declaration of Independence. It was destroyed. He had burned it. He whispered, "The Declaration."

Grumbles and murmurs spread throughout the room.

Kat gasped. She knew if she didn't get all of these men to sign the Declaration before the end of the day, there would be no 4th of July. "How are you going to sign the Declaration? You have to sign it today!"

Everyone looked to Mr. Jefferson. "I don't see how that is possible, young lady."

"No!" Kat screamed. "You HAVE to!"

The room stirred at Kat's bold and demanding tone.

Kat remembered where she was and calmed her voice. "I mean, sir, that I don't mean to be disrespectful, but I know you can find a way to sign it today. It's the 4th of July."

JQ leaned over to Kat. "I think we all know the date, Kat," he whispered.

Thomas Jefferson walked to Kat and said, "We unfortunately will not be able to continue with the signing unless this document is rewritten, Miss McGee, and at this moment, that can not happen. I need my notes, and the men who helped me will need theirs. It takes time. We will need to begin anew. I am sorry. I'm afraid it would be impossible."

In that moment, Liberty's voice echoed in Kat's head: *It will make the impossible seem possible.*

Kat stood up straight and said, "Well, Mr. Jefferson, I happen to believe in miracles." She only hoped this one would work.

CHAPTER 10
TRAPPED IN TIME

The ashes and charred remaining bits of the Declaration of Independence sat on the table in front of Kat. As she pulled Liberty's torch out of her backpack, she felt an uneasy sense of pressure.

Only the most important men in the history of the United States were standing behind her, counting on her, Kat McGee, to save their treasured document. Her hands were sweaty like the time her entire Totsville Tiger track team was relying on her to grab the baton in the last leg of the relay race to bring home the county-wide championship win . . . and she dropped it.

Oh jeez, Kat thought. *Please don't fail me now, dear torch.*

JQ, Paul Revere, and Thomas Jefferson had witnessed the magic of the torch pick them up and whisk them in a translucent bubble from the Freedom Fort back to Philadelphia, so they were expecting another astonishing spectacle to unfold in front of their eyes. The rest of the crowd peered over Kat's shoulders with curious stares.

Kat heard the clock ticking behind her. Tick, tock. Tick tock. She pointed the torch at the ruined document, and concentrated.

Nothing.

"Why do we listen to a child?" A man shouted from the back of the room. "Nothing is happening!" another shouted. Mr. Jefferson hushed them immediately.

Kat tried to forget the comment, but the man was right. It wasn't working. Something was wrong with the torch.

JQ leaned over to Kat. "You did it once, Kat. You can do it again."

But that was just it. Kat wasn't sure *what* she had done to make the magic torch take them away, and once they had landed in Philadelphia the torch had stopped and shrunk, as if it had run out of juice. She closed her eyes and tried to concentrate as she had done before.

Kat thought about the importance of the Declaration of Independence and its impact on their country.

Still nothing.

Kat had another worrisome thought. If the torch didn't work, not only would she fail, she would be stuck here. Liberty had said the torch would lead her home. Although she had enjoyed her adventure with JQ and Paul Revere and Thomas Jefferson, she wanted to go home. She didn't want to be stuck in 1776.

The men in the room became restless. Suddenly everyone was shouting at each other again.

"The congress should start fresh."

"We are wasting time on a child's fantasy!"

"No, let the girl try again!"

"This is serious business, not a game of make-believe!"

Kat knew fighting about it wasn't going to help anything. "STOP!" she yelled.

"The torch can bring us all together; I've seen it happen. But we need to be open-minded and support each other instead of arguing!" Kat was surprised at her own confidence and conviction.

Mr. Jefferson stepped forward. "The girl is correct. If we were able to unite on the purpose and importance of the Declaration, we need to find that solidarity again."

The men gathered around Kat and leaned toward the torch, which Kat pointed directly at the Declaration of Independence.

"I need your support, so please, come closer. Let's close our eyes, and think about what this document means for us, for our country, and for the future," Kat said. She didn't know if any of this would make a difference, but at this point she would try anything.

Paul Revere was the first to do it. JQ and Jefferson followed. And one by one, the men in the circle put their arms on the next man's back, and the group was soon in a gigantic group hug.

Kat smiled. That was more like it.

Kat squeezed the handle of the torch and said, "Okay. Let's close our eyes."

A man whispered, "This is poppycock!"

"Hush," another admonished.

"We need to concentrate—together," Kat said. "Think of the most important values this document represents."

Jefferson whispered, "Freedom."

JQ said, "Responsibility."

Paul Revere leaned forward. "Liberty."

Ben Franklin said, "Equality."

Around the circle, men whispered, "Dignity . . . independence . . . strength . . . hope . . . fairness . . . union . . . progress . . ."

The torch gently sputtered in Kat's hand, coming to life. It vibrated slightly and enlarged and illuminated slowly, first the handle, then the torch. It was dim but as each person spoke, the torch brightened, as if it felt the tension disappear and gained strength from the emotion in the room.

Kat opened her eyes as the energy in her hand intensified, and she felt that same force that lifted their group off the ground at the Freedom Fort. This time, a small beam of light shot out from the end of the torch, like a laser at one of those cool space shows at the Totsville Science Center.

Kat pointed the ray of light toward the ashes of the Declaration of Independence. As if someone had pressed a rewind button, the ashes turned back to paper, and the document began to piece itself back together.

"It's happening!" Kat exclaimed.

The men in the circle began opening their eyes, and they couldn't believe what they saw. There was no trace that the document had ever been torched.

"I have witnessed a miracle!"

"The Declaration lives!"

"We will have our independence!"

The men jumped up and down without unlocking their arms; a giant circle of grown men pounded the floor and shouted together.

"Hip, hip, hooray!"

"Hooray for Kat McGee!"

Everyone threw his arms in the air, and Kat was lifted and paraded around the room as if she had just scored a winning goal. As she flew around the room, feeling ecstatic and proud, she accidentally knocked her hand against a beam close to the ceiling.

Before Kat knew what happened, Liberty's torch fell out of her hands.

CRASH!

SPLAT!

The torch hit the hard, wooden floor and shattered to pieces.

The celebration stopped. Kat was lowered to the floor and ran to the broken torch.

"No. Way," Kat said, astonished at what lay in front of her.

Pieces of Liberty's torch were scattered all over the floor.

Kat's mouth started trembling. "That was my ticket home."

The forefathers gathered the pieces of the torch and handed them to Kat. Thomas Jefferson stepped forward. "Perhaps we can mend it?" Even he did not sound convinced.

Kat shook her head. "Continue with the plan. You need to sign the Declaration of Independence."

"There will be time for that, young lady," Paul Revere said.

The men shuffled their feet, murmuring. No one knew what to do.

Then a small voice came from the corner of the room. "Perhaps I can help."

Everyone in the room turned toward the voice.

Romulus Rulerwink, hands still tied behind his back, struggled to stand. "I may have an idea."

The group was skeptical.

JQ asked, "What could *you* do?"

Romulus offered, "As I said, I am a scientist and alchemist. I may be able to mix a potion to put your torch together again."

Kat said, "What, like glue? I don't think glue is going to do the trick."

"What's glue?" JQ asked, looking at Kat.

"You don't know what glue is?" Kat asked incredulously.

Romulus shrugged. "I know not of glue, but I know a mixture that serves as an adhesive. I would only need a few household chemicals we can gather quickly and easily."

Mr. Jefferson said, "Give us a list and we'll send a messenger to gather the ingredients. You can do it here I presume?"

Romulus nodded. He dictated a list to a couple of young men Jefferson had summoned, and they were on their way.

"In the meantime," Kat said. "We need to get that document signed."

Mr. Adams agreed, "It is necessary, Mr. Jefferson."

Jefferson and Adams gathered the men of the Continental Congress and began signing their most important document. Kat was worried about the torch, but was so happy to see the Declaration signed that she almost forgot that she had no way back to the present.

The young messengers soon returned with the ingredients for the adhesive, and they temporarily untied Rulerwink's hands so he could mix them, keeping a close eye on him all the while.

As the final few signatures were placed on the Declaration, Romulus dipped each piece of the torch in his concoction and placed them back together. Kat ran and grabbed it from him.

Please, please, please, Kat thought. *Tell me where I should go to get home.*

The torch was still and dull.

The men turned to Rulerwink, who shrugged again. "I didn't say it would work. I know not how to travel through time."

Kat slumped to the floor. None of it mattered if she couldn't get home. She'd never be able to celebrate the 4th of July again. She suddenly could hardly breathe. What was she going to do in 1776? What about her family? Why would Liberty let something like this happen? Certainly there was another way.

Kat continued to point the torch in different directions. Everyone in the room came close to her, and they tried to repeat what they had experienced before.

Nothing. The torch was done.

JQ shook his head. "I'm so sorry Kat. If it weren't for you, I'd still be writing my punishment on the board."

Kat looked at JQ. It came to them both at the same time. "THE CHALKBOARD!"

JQ shouted, "I'll race you there!"

The two kids ran out of the room, down the hall, up the stairs, and around another hall with every member of the congress trailing them. They piled into the room with the chalkboard where JQ had found Kat hiding in the closet not two days ago.

"I will not disobey my parents," Kat said, reciting JQ's lines on the board. "Thanks, JQ. You may have found my way home."

JQ smiled, but was curious. "So how are you going to make this chalkboard transport you like the one in Libertyland?"

Kat smiled, remembering Gram's words about magic: *the belief in the impossible and the unknowable, serendipitous circumstances . . . the perfect pinch of a plethora of ingredients stirred to-*

gether. "I have to believe. This is how I got here. I just have to hope Liberty's watching from the other side and will help me . . . even though I broke her torch." Kat frowned.

Kat picked up a piece of chalk, an eraser, and handed them to JQ. "Will you erase your words and write July 4, 2014?" JQ took the chalk and nodded.

Kat looked out over the room as the members of the congress began to gather, and she walked to Thomas Jefferson and Paul Revere. "I won't ever forget my time here. Thank you."

Mr. Adams stepped forward. "Thank you, Miss McGee, for helping to recover two of our most prized possessions. I am so proud of you, and I know my son has learned a great deal from you."

Kat said, "I have to say, I have learned from him too! He is so dedicated to your cause and wants to help in any and every way he can." She looked at JQ, who blushed. "That's one smart fellow, and I'm proud to say a friend."

John Adams turned to his son and smiled. "He has proven to be both capable and intuitive. Perhaps he should accompany me to Paris?" Mr. Adams winked at JQ.

JQ beamed. He ran up and bowed deeply to Kat. "You have inspired me, Miss Kat McGee. This is the best time I have had in my life."

Kat patted JQ's shoulder. "Oh, you have a lot more ahead of you to look forward to." JQ's eyes widened. Kat smiled. "And one of these days, I'm going to race you and win."

She turned to Mr. Jefferson and Paul Revere and curtsied. "Thank you, sirs, for all that you have done and all you will continue to do. I owe everything to you." Kat smiled, realizing how polite and formal her words were—1776 had rubbed off on her.

Mr. Jefferson smiled down. "Miss McGee, our future is in great hands if you are emblematic of the children of your era. Thank you for your lesson."

"Lesson?" Kat asked.

"You taught us to believe in possibilities even when hope seems lost, and your courage showed us what can happen when one stays true to herself and the ideals she believes in. You showed great maturity and responsibility. In matters of principle, we must all stand like a rock. "

Kat blushed. *Man, I wish Gram and Miss Libby could see me now*. With that, she turned toward the chalkboard, closed her eyes, and thought of home. It was time to get back where she belonged.

CHAPTER 11

A NEW AND IMPROVED LIVING MUSEUM

Time seemed to stand still as Kat stared at the chalkboard. She tried not to doubt, but fully, totally, and completely convince herself that this board would take her home.

Kat thought of her family: Gram baking apple pie popovers, Gus and Abe playing in the backyard, Hannah painting her nails, Emily on her iPad, Ben and Polly fighting in the backseat of the minivan. She saw all of them together at the Totsville 4th of July Parade, waving sparklers and watching the floats go by, and she felt as if she were there, as if she could reach out and touch the nearest float . . .

Kat squeezed the pieced-back-together torch in one hand and reached her other hand out toward her family and her daydream and the squishy sensation traveled up her arm to her shoulder. Kat wiggled her fingers and tried to reach further into the goo, and she finally felt that tug and—

WHOOSH!

Kat was yanked through the board and heard a round of goodbyes trailing behind her. This ride was a little bumpier than her first, as if she were tumbling in the non-delicate cycle of a washing machine, but Kat grabbed her knees and curled into a ball and tossed and tumbled her way back to the present.

Kat smiled from ear-to-ear the entire time.

When Kat opened her eyes, her spirit deflated.

It didn't work.

She must have landed in another strange time because all she saw was a tree of eyeballs with long skinny branches in front of her. Kat blinked: more eyeballs. But as she sat up and blinked again and again and focused, the branches became arms and the eyeballs were actually on faces.

It wasn't a tree of eyeballs at all. Kat was surrounded by people.

"She's awake! She's coming to!" A woman shouted.

The crowd of unfamiliar faces parted like a river and a large green figure approached, running toward Kat.

Liberty!

Kat breathed a huge sigh of relief.

"Oh Kat! You made it! We were so worried!" Liberty grinned happily and turned toward the crowd. "She's okay. Kat made it!"

Someone started to clap and soon the entire crowd was roaring in applause for Kat.

Kat felt her head and arms and legs, and thankfully her body appeared to be in one piece.

Liberty took Kat's hand and helped her stand. "Some people have been known to break bones on reentry, so I'm glad your fingers and toes didn't get caught on anything that wouldn't let go."

Kat shivered but smiled. "But, is this the present? Am I in Libertyland?"

"Oh, yes, you were very focused, so you landed in the present part of Libertyland instead of the chalkboards of change. Come with me. I have some people who are very anxious to see you."

As Liberty pulled Kat out of the room, the woman who first shouted patted her on the back. Was that Elizabeth Taylor? As Kat stepped over the threshold into the hallway she could have sworn she saw Michael Jackson showing Steve Jobs the moon-walk.

Kat saw Liberty's torch pulling them down the hallway.

"Wait. But I broke your torch. What is that?"

Liberty looked back at Kat, eyes twinkling, a big grin on her face. "Oh, sweetie. That was my travel torch. It's handier because I can fit it anywhere, but it isn't nearly as sturdy, as you found out. Not to worry, my dear. Not to worry."

Phew! Kat had been scared to break the news to Liberty. She was relieved.

Liberty and Kat had barely stepped through the doorway of the American Revolution room when a throng of people rushed over to greet her.

"The lady of the hour!"

"It's Kat McGee! She's here!"

"Hip, hip, hooray!"

Kat felt like she had never left.

Liberty pushed through the crowd to a table. The table held the Declaration of Independence. Kat looked down and saw all 56 signatures.

Kat turned and looked out and saw the frozen people on the other side of the Libertyland. But instead of an empty display case, she saw the Declaration of Independence, safe below the glass, people peering inside. She didn't see her siblings and turned to ask Liberty where they were.

Instead of Liberty, Thomas Jefferson was in front of her. Kat looked in his eyes and saw the same fire she first noticed at the Freedom Fort.

"A pleasure to see you again, Miss McGee," Mr. Jefferson said to Kat.

Kat curtsied. "The pleasure is all mine, sir. You are looking well."

Jefferson nodded, "I can't move as nimbly, but I am feeling fit as a fiddle."

Kat felt a nudge in her back and turned around. She didn't recognize the man in front of her, but he was smiling as if they were the best of friends.

I'm sure I'm supposed to know what famous person in history this is, Kat thought. *But I don't.*

The man said, "Wanna race?"

Kat threw her arms around the big man. "JQ! You're all grown up!"

"Well, I'm not usually in this part of Libertyland, but I heard you were going to be here, so I asked Liberty permission to come over for a spell," JQ explained.

Kat beamed. "I'm very glad you did."

"I, too, asked for permission to come and see you," a soft voice said from behind.

Kat turned and was shocked to see the man standing in front of her.

"You helped me see the error of my ways," he said. "May I express my thanks in a hug?"

Kat looked at Liberty, then back at the man. She nodded.

Romulus Rulerwink walked over and hugged Kat.

"I paid my penance, learned my lesson, and reformed myself," Romulus explained.

Liberty added, "And he is here for something very special he invented many years after your unfortunate first encounter."

Rulerwink pulled a bottle from behind his back to show Kat.

Kat read the label: RULERGLUE.

"I wanted to make sure young people would always be able to put things back together again," Rulerwink said.

"That's wonderful!" Kat exclaimed.

"Romulus has been very helpful in the maintenance and up-keep of Libertyland as well," Liberty added. "We all rely on him quite frequently."

Rulerwink dropped his head, blushing. "I simply realized the importance of taking responsibility for one's actions and working together. Most importantly, I learned what freedom truly means."

"Here, here!" John Adams yelled.

"HERE, HERE!" the room repeated.

Kat threw up her hands and yelled, "Here, here!"

Now this, Kat thought, *is what Libertyland is all about.*

Kat was happy and sad at once. She said her goodbyes to her friends in 1776 and promised to return soon. The icons in 1776 continued their independence celebration, and the others headed to their respective places in Libertyland. JQ slipped back to the space with other United States Presidents, and Romulus went back to the world of 18TH century inventors.

Liberty and her torch guided Kat back to the empty room where Kat had first arrived in Libertyland; it seemed like an eternity ago, but she had left only two days earlier.

"Can't I stay? I want to see all of Libertyland! I want to meet and hang out with these famous Americans a little longer," Kat begged.

"But you'll miss the 4th of July! I thought for sure you would want to see the results of your handiwork," Liberty said.

Kat knew she wanted to see her family, but how could she leave this wondrous place?

Kat and Liberty stood in front of the nondescript door with a star-shaped doorknob. Liberty turned to Kat. "Although the world may never know what you did, here in Libertyland we will always know and appreciate it," Liberty said, smiling.

Kat threw her arms around the gigantic green-gowned goddess and squeezed. "Thank you, Liberty . . . for everything." Without looking up because she didn't want to cry, Kat turned and grabbed hold of the star, before she could change her mind.

Kat McGee, you saved America was all Kat heard as she was sucked into darkness.

Kat opened her eyes and found herself standing in a crowd of people. She pushed her way to the display case and saw it: the Declaration of Independence. Kat peered more closely and squinted; she could barely make out a charcoal line in the corner, as if a tiny part had been burned.

Kat looked up at the glass display behind the case containing the heroes of the Revolutionary War and smiled, knowing that behind that glass, those statues were not still or lifeless at all.

"Come on, Kat. What are you still doing in here?"

Kat felt a tug at her shoulder; it was her sister Polly. "We've been here for hours and have been all over the museum!" Polly pulled Kat back through the crowd to the door, where her other siblings were waiting impatiently.

"Gram said we can go home!" Gus yelled, a little too loudly. Museum patrons turned and hushed them. In an exaggerated whisper Gus continued, "We're not going to miss the 4th of July in Totsville! Hurry up!"

"What do you mean?" Kat asked. "Today *is* the 4th of July."

Hannah sighed. "Oh, Kat. Always in your own little world. We just got here."

Kat remembered Liberty's words on her first day in Libertyland, *They don't even know you're gone.* Could it be? Did she simply dream of her adventures the last two days in 1776? Or did Liberty send her back to the exact moment she left?

"We'll need to hurry if we want to make it back to Totsville tonight," Gram's loving voice came from behind Kat. Kat turned and saw the familiar sparkle in her eyes.

"So there is a 4th of July after all?" Kat asked.

"Why wouldn't there be?" Gram said, ushering the McGee kids toward the exit. "Of course there's a 4th of July. You should know that better than anyone, Kool Kat."

As her siblings ran toward the minivan parked outside, Kat gave Gram a huge bear hug. "Thank you, Gram."

Gram pulled away and leaned down to Kat. "No," she whispered. "Thank *you*."

CHAPTER 12

FIREWORKS IN TOTSVILLE

Kat McGee, you saved America! Kat McGee, you saved America! The words echoed in Kat's head, and she felt supremely happy daydreaming of her time in Libertyland and 1776 as she headed toward the POFF headquarters on the morning of July 4th.

The McGees were unusually quiet and subdued, napping on and off all the way home from Philadelphia, and the kids drowsily climbed out of bed the next day for the citywide baseball tournament and tractor pull. The ice cream sundae contest was a blast; Kat had eaten so much she still felt full.

Kat was still in a daze from their trip, but it was finally here: July 4th and the Parade of Floats and Fireworks. Kat knew she was going to do her best to help with the POFF, regardless of what Roman Rule would make her do.

Kylie Kaitlyn, one of Roman's third grade minions, startled Kat out of her daydream as Kat pulled her bike into the parking lot of the school's gym, where the floats were always held before the parade. "Thank goodness you're here! You've got to come look at this float! The motor isn't working and it's not going to make it on time! Do something! Kat McGee, save the parade!"

Kat quickly got off her bike and focused. A distraught Kylie shoved the POFF clipboard into Kat's hands. She looked around.

All of the floats were in line and ready to go out the garage-like door that opened into the driveway behind the school. But the American Heroine float was not among the others. Kat guessed this was the cause of the nervous third-grader's panic.

Kylie handed a walkie-talkie to Kat. Kat was confused—Roman should fix this issue, not her. But the POFF needed Kat's help, so she would give it to them.

Kat flew into POFF organizational mode: She called the maintenance guru, Tito Tubberville, who was on call to help with any float emergency. Tito arrived in a flash and immediately set about to fix the American Heroine float motor. Within minutes, he had the motor humming like a songbird.

Kat saw that the lineup needed changing.

"Kylie, inform Mr. Fisher that the American Heroine float will follow them instead of going before them."

Kylie knew Mr. Fisher was incredibly Type A when it came to his John Carroll Marching Band. She hesitated. "But . . . "

"Don't think," Kat interrupted. "Just do it. Trust me." She knew Mr. Fisher was a good guy and would forgive her eventually.

Kat informed the rest of the POFF through her walkie-talkie of the rearranged lineup, and the floats began to move through the door without a hitch. She had avoided a potentially devastating traffic jam. Kat breathed a sigh of relief and looked around her.

The Parade of Floats and Fireworks was in full swing. But why were Kylie and Tito looking to Kat as if she were in charge? She had to find Miss Libby. Maybe she could explain.

As Kat turned around she ran right into none other than Roman Rule.

"Hello, McGee," Roman said snidely.

Kat cowered back initially, but recovered and held her head high, remembering what she had learned in 1776. She had nothing to be ashamed or afraid of. "Hi Roman. What's up?" She was determined to keep her composure, regardless of how horrible Roman was going to be to her.

But much to her surprise, Roman smiled. "Nice job with the Heroine float, McGee. I was a little worried, but you made a call and took care of business. I appreciate it."

Kat practically fell out of her sneakers she was so shocked. What? Was this her nemesis?

Roman put his hand on Kat's shoulder. "Are you okay? Do you need Kylie to relieve you for five minutes? We still have a long day ahead, and I can't do it without you, McGee."

Kat opened her mouth but no sound came out. Finally she was able to speak. "No, no. I'm fine."

"Great. I'll radio you when we need to start getting the fireworks set up," Roman said, patting her back and walking away.

Kylie stood next to Kat like a lost puppy and smiled. "Anything I can do for you Kat? Do you need me to run an errand or help you in any other way?"

Kat tried to shake off her dazed and confused feeling. "I'm fine now. Thanks, Kylie."

Kat turned and looked down the street where the floats and bands and cars and clowns inched along the route. Out in the distance she saw her brothers and sisters smiling and laughing and eating and having a great time.

"Actually, Kylie, give me five minutes. I'll be right back," Kat said, shoving the clipboard in an amazed Kylie's hands.

Before Kylie could argue, Kat ran down the road to the Mc-Gee family spot on the edge of the street.

Polly ran up to her first. "This is the best parade EVER! Congrats, Kat!"

Gus and Abe were busy eating cotton candy and she couldn't hear them over the band that was passing by, but they both gave her a thumbs up.

Gram sat behind them all, content in the same folding chair she took to Abe's Little League games, Ben's mini-golf tournaments, and Emily's violin concerts, smiling and soaking it all in.

Hannah, sitting beside Gram and reading *War and Peace*, looked up. "So how was your big debut as POFF student ambassador? Shouldn't you be ordering people around right now?"

Kat looked at Gram. "Um . . . yeah. I mean, yes. I'm really busy. I just got confused. Gram?"

Gram stood up and handed Kat her backpack. "You left this in the minivan the other night. I thought you might need it." Gram sat back down with a wink in Kat's general direction.

"Keyhole to Padlock. We need you in the staging area, STAT. Repeat. Keyhole to Padlock," Kat's walkie-talkie boomed from her pocket.

Kat grabbed her backpack, waved, and yelled back at her family, "I'll be back as soon as I can! Will see you at the fireworks!"

Kat ran back to the float staging area where Kylie ran in with the clipboard. Roman gathered all the parade volunteers around him. "Nice job so far, folks.

Kat is going to take the A-team over to the field to make sure all the fireworks are ready to roll. B-team, stay with me to finish up here. I do believe this is the best POFF ever, and that's because we did it together!" The group cheered and dispersed. The members of the POFF committee waved from down the street and smiled.

As Kat's team headed over to the field, Kat stayed behind and approached Roman. He was watching the final float, Paul Revere on his horse lighting a lantern, like a proud father.

He looked at Kat. "Can you believe we pulled this off, McGee? Everyone keeps telling me this has been the best parade in years. You should be proud."

Kat nodded hesitantly. "Yeah, um, sure. Thanks for the opportunity?"

"Opportunity? Whatever! You earned it and deserved it. We're a team, McGee. I'm glad we compromised and worked together as co-ambassadors. It was so much better."

Kat was still astonished. Team? Compromise? Working together? Did Liberty change everything when she was gone? Or was she really gone?

Roman pointed to the Paul Revere impersonator. "You know I have a distant relative who knew Paul Revere."

Kat smiled. "Really? How?"

"Oh, my great-great-great-grandfather. He's the one who invented this thing called Rulerglue. You can hardly find it anymore, but legend in the Rule family is that he knew Paul Revere and Thomas Jefferson and a bunch of the founding fathers. I don't know, but my grandfather says I remind him of old Rulerwink."

Kat almost spit out her kettle corn. "Did you say Rulerwink?"

"Yeah," Roman said. "My family shortened the name later down the line—my great-grandfather hated the name Rulerwink. Anyway, I'll catch up with you at the field in a bit. Go enjoy the end of the parade with your family. I know you want to."

"You do?" Kat asked.

"Well, yeah, you keep talking about how important it is to you. That's cool. I think it's a good thing. But I'll meet you at five o'clock. Miss Libby will meet us there with the pyro staff. See you in a bit!" Before Kat could respond Roman ran off.

Kat stood still, watching her family and her town enjoy the end of the parade. She peeked inside her backpack and all she saw was a small glowing stick the size of a pen.

Really? Kat thought.

Kat looked both ways and pulled out the stick, but it wasn't a stick. There, with a few cracks, was the miniature of Liberty's torch.

Roman Rule was being not only friendly, but *cool* to her. She was a co-student ambassador on the POFF committee. Her family was being nice to her. And it was the 4th of July in Totsville.

Could it be true? Could she have really gone back in time and spent two days with Thomas Jefferson, John Quincy Adams, and Paul Revere? Was it possible that Libertyland was a real place and she shook hands with famous icons and saw a changed Rulerwink become a part of American history?

The United States was alive and well. Totsville was celebrating independence, freedom and equality, and Kat had seen compromise and dignity and hope all around her in just a few minutes. Was it possible it hadn't been a dream at all?

As Kat held the miniature torch in her hand it shined brightly.

That was the sign she needed. In this world, Kat had changed her own little piece of history. And that was all that mattered.

Liberty stepped back from her looking bell proudly, watching Kat and Roman work on the Totsville Parade of Floats and Fireworks in the glow of the bell.

The torch guided Liberty down to the chalkboards of change, and she was pulled to the end of the room, where a blank chalkboard hung amidst the famous dates in American history.

Liberty reached up to the blank chalkboard and wrote:

JULY 4TH, 2014: KAT MCGEE SAVES AMERICA

That Kat McGee, Liberty thought. *She really knows how to holiday.*

ACKNOWLEDGMENTS

I'd like to thank Carey Albertine and Saira Rao for all they are doing to make great books about real girls and inviting me to the party. Thanks to Nick Guarracino and Kati Robins for complementing Kat's journey with amazing illustrations and thoughtful guides. To the interns at ITTM for your fresh, smart approach to aid my social media sluggishness. Thanks to Genevieve Gagne-Hawes for her insight and always helping me to elevate Kat and her story. Thanks to the friends, family, students, and teachers who came out and supported Kat (and me) on our first tour. To my family, near and far; wish we could see you more. And to my husband, for reading draft after draft and giving me wonderful feedback—even when I don't seem to want to hear it, I need and appreciate it immensely. Kat saves America—you save me.

Jeremiah 29:11

About Kristin Riddick

Kristin Riddick does not currently possess the ability to travel through time . . . except in her imagination. And, like Kat, she never met an adventure she didn't like. She has acted in commercials, sitcoms, webisodes, and her husband's iPhone road trip movies. Her voice can be heard on television and in films, but you will never know it is hers so it seems very mysterious. She teaches Pilates and spinning to stay sane, and because she thinks it puts people in better moods. A native of Corpus Christi, Texas, Kristin graduated from The University of Virginia and currently divides her time between Los Angeles and Austin with another amazing adventurer, her husband.

Also by Kristin Riddick – *Kat McGee and the Halloween Costume Caper*

Coming soon- *Kat McGee and the Thanksgiving Turkey Train*

Connect with Kristin
www.kristinriddick.com
www.facebook.com/AKatMcgeeAdventure
twitter: @katmcgeebooks

Reading Guide
By Kati Robins

CHAPTER 1: Summer Bummer

Vocabulary Words: indelible, self-esteem, accomplished, ambassador, responsibility, pretentious, menaced, logical, curmudgeon, regal, tyrannical, sauntered, snide, serendipitous, plethora, reluctantly, betrayed

Discussion Questions:

1. What does Kat McGee love most about summer? _____

2. What is Kat's unfortunate nickname, and how did she get it?

_____

3. How many brothers and sisters does Kat have? _____

4. What made Kat feel like she belonged among her accomplished siblings? _____

_____

5. What does "too big for her britches" mean? _____

_____

6. A lot of kids didn't believe Kat when she told stories about her adventures. Have you ever been told that you "made something up", or been called a liar? If so, how did it make you feel? _____

_____

7. "Anjali was a good friend who didn't care what other kids said about Kat." What lesson did Anjali remind Kat of? _____

_____

8. What grade is Kat in? _____

9. What responsibilities would the student ambassador be in charge of? _____

_____

_____

10. Who was the only person standing between Kat and her rightful position as POFF student ambassador? _____

11. Describe Roman Rule. _____

_____

12. Who was Kat's only unconditional ally? _____

13. Emily told Kat not to be a "sore loser." Do you think Kat is being a sore loser? Explain. _____

_____

14. According to Gram, what makes magic? _____

_____

_____

15. Where is Gram taking all of the kids, and why? _____

_____

_____

16. In this chapter, Gram says, "Those who don't know history are destined to repeat it." What does this statement mean? ___

_____

_____

Activities:

Create a character journal that includes three columns: Character Name, Facts and Characteristics, and Portrait. Each time you meet a new character, add their name to the journal. As you read and get to know each of them, list details about their lives, their families, their physical characteristics, and their personality traits. Then draw a portrait of each character.

Create a flyer, or brochure, advertising the 4th of July Festival. Use the description in this chapter to include as many events and details as possible.

The American Heroine float would carry people dressed as Sacajawea, Susan B. Anthony, and Betsy Ross. Label an index card for each of these American heroines. On one side of the index card paste or draw a picture of the heroine, and on the other side of the index card list 5 interesting facts about her, or reasons why she is an American heroine.

Social Studies connection: The Revolution float would have a Paul Revere impersonator. Dress up as Paul Revere and recite *The*

Midnight Ride of Paul Revere by Henry Wadsworth Longfellow in front of your class, or family.

Science connection: The Moon Landing Float would display a fake meteor shower made with sparklers. Create your own model of a meteor shower using something other than sparklers, and present it to your class.

Do some research to find out who is credited with saying "Those who don't know history are destined to repeat it."

CHAPTER 2: Libertyland

Vocabulary Words: quizzically, throng, renovation, mischievous, gravitated, effervescence, threshold, stoic, hence, apparition, inconceivable, orator, expectantly

Discussion Questions:

1. "Everyone was mad at Kat and on a short fuse." What does "short fuse" mean?

_____

2. When Kat realizes that her ticket is different than everyone else's, what does Gram tell her? _____

_____

3. When Kat inserts her ticket into the mysterious door and is transported into an empty room, who is standing there to meet her? _____

4. What is the All-American Girls Baseball League? _____

_____

5. What is Libertyland? _____

What does *living museum* mean? _____

_____

6. What is wrong in the Revolutionary War room? _____

_____

_____

7. Why is it so important for Kat to help find Thomas Jefferson and the Declaration of Independence? _____

_____

_____

8. Who do you think is to blame for the disappearance of Thomas Jefferson and the Declaration of Independence? _____

Activities:

Kat said that Liberty was "the tallest woman she had ever seen." How tall is the actual Statue of Liberty? _____
Be sure to use a reliable Internet source for your information and list the website here:

_____

Using mossy, green colored clay, sculpt your own replica of the Statue of Liberty.

"Willie Mays, Jackie Robinson, and Ty Cobb were eating a hot dog on a set of bleachers." Read some history about each of these baseball players; then, construct a conversation that they would have been having together on the bleachers. Act out the conversation for your class.

Create a guidebook for Libertyland. As Liberty leads Kat through each room of the living museum, write down and describe all of the events, icons, foods, and music that she encounters. For example, your "American Baseball" page would include facts and descriptions about Babe Ruth, Joe DiMaggio, Willie Mays, Ty Cobb, Hank Aaron, Jackie Robinson, and the All-American Girls Baseball League; and your "Wild West" page would include facts and descriptions about Will Rogers, John Wayne, Gene Autry, and Buffalo Bill. Create a page for each room of the museum.

CHAPTER 3: Liberty's Looking Bell

Vocabulary List: luminous, bleak, democracy, snarky, improbable

Discussion Questions:

1. What is the looking bell? _____

_____

2. Who is Rulerwink? _____

_____

3. What does Miss Libby's Spanish name, Libertad, mean in English? _____

4. What are the two things that Kat knows for sure? _____

_____

_____

_____

5. Who does Rulerwink remind Kat of? _____

Activities:

Draw a picture depicting July 4, 2029 in Rulerworld using the description in this chapter.

In this chapter, Kat says that if she "had not helped Dolce because she was nervous or not ridden the sleigh because she was scared, none of those adventures would have happened! She never would have been able to meet Cookie Crocodile in the Swamp of Sorrows. She and Sadie Claus never would have saved Santa from Scoogie sending him to the South Pole!" If you haven't already, read the other books in the Kat McGee series, *Kat McGee and the Halloween Costume Caper* and *Kat McGee and the School of Christmas Spirit*, and learn about Kat's other wildly imaginative adventures.

CHAPTER 4: Through the Chalkboard of Change

Vocabulary List: prevail, stature, angular, spindly, civilized

Discussion Questions:

1. What does *infamy* mean? _____

_____

2. Which date and event did Kat want to know more about? __

_____

3. Describe what you think "three days of peace and music" would be like. _____

_____

_____

4. What can the *Chalkboards of Change* do? _____

_____

_____

Activities:

Create a timeline starting from 1492 – present day and fill in all of the important dates and events that are mentioned in the story. Include two interesting facts about each event.

CHAPTER 5: An Enlightened Journey

Vocabulary List: enlightened, ornate, indecent, stern, petticoats, parasols, tailcoats, urgency, contend, gravely, rebellion,

Discussion Questions:

1. Where is Kat at the beginning of this chapter? _____

_____

   2. Why hadn't the little boy that Kat met ever shaken a girl's hand before? _____

_____

3. Kat felt like a "fish out of water." What does this saying mean? _____

_____

4. Why did John get in trouble? _____

_____

_____

5. Why does Kat think that it is so cool that the dress John got for her came from Betsy Ross? _____

_____

6. Who is John's father? _____

7. Why does JQ want to help Kat? _____

_____

_____

Activities:

Research John Quincy Adams' life (http://www.history.com/top-ics/us-presidents/john-quincy-adams) and create a presentation on his road to the Presidency. Include facts about his early life and his career as a diplomat and politician.

CHAPTER 6: Continental What?

Vocabulary List: diligently, incredulously, wavered, prudent, decipher, culprit, provisions, paraphernalia, distraught, sentimental, inquisitive, dutiful, pertinent,

Discussion Questions:

1. What is the Continental Congress, and why does JQ care so much about it? _____

_____

_____

_____

2. Where had Kat seen Benjamin Franklin's face before? _____

_____

3. What is Rulerwink's plan? _____

_____

_____

4. What do you think Rulerwink's cryptic message means, and where do you think he is hiding Thomas Jefferson? _____

_____

_____

5. Who is JQ's friend that they are going to find, and why do you think he'll be helpful to them? _____

_____

Activities:

Research Benjamin Franklin's many inventions. discoveries, and improvements (http://www.ushistory.org/franklin/info/inventions.htm) and create a PowerPoint presentation that includes a slide for each.

CHAPTER 7: The Second Midnight Ride of Paul Revere

Vocabulary List: rustic, commodity, famished, ironic, gruesome, flippantly, dapper, intrigued, furrowed, chutzpah, traitorous, laboriously, toiled, interject, perplexed, convenes, predicament

Discussion Questions:

1. Why does Kat think that summer in 1776 would be boring?

_____

_____

Do you agree, or disagree with her? Explain. _____

_____

2. What is the Freedom Fort, and what is it used for? _____

_____

_____

3. Why does JQ believe that Paul Revere is the only adult who will help them?

_____

_____

4. How has Paul Revere helped the cause? _____

_____

_____

5. Why does Kat wish that she had asked for an iPhone for Christmas? _____

_____

Activities:

Using a Venn diagram, compare and contrast life in 1776 to life today.

Visit The Paul Revere House (http://www.paulreverehouse.org/ride/) to learn more about Paul Revere's famous midnight ride.

CHAPTER 8: A Spell at the State House

Vocabulary List: instinctively, persevere, disintegrated, confronting, fraud, gaunt, stupor, immense,

Discussion Questions:

1. Explain what Thomas Jefferson meant by the following statements.

"Action is what defines us." _____

_____

_____

"We must persevere, but remain calm. Nothing gives one person so much advantage over another as to remain always cool and unruffled under all circumstances."

_____

_____

_____

"One man, or woman, in this case, with courage is a majority."

_____

_____

Activities:

Research famous quotes made by Thomas Jefferson. Which one is your favorite, and why? _____

_____

_____

Create a poster illustrating the differences between a monarchy and a democracy.

CHAPTER 9: Life, Liberty, and the Pursuit of Romulus

Vocabulary List: combative, tyrant, alchemist, concocted, respect, compromise, dignity

Discussion Questions:

1. Why did Romulus devise this evil plan? _____

_____

2. Kat knew what it felt like to want recognition. Have you ever been in a position, or situation, where you wanted recognition and didn't get it? Explain.

_____

_____

3. What does Romulus Rulerwink say in this chapter to prove that he is not a man of strong character or integrity? _____

_____

4. How does JQ define *freedom*? _____

_____

_____

5. As she listened to Thomas Jefferson and John Adams, what did Kat realize about herself and her own behavior? _____

_____

6. What lesson did Kat learn? _____

_____

7. What vision did the Founding Fathers have for this nation?

_____

Activities:

Research The Declaration of Independence. Find out who helped draft it, how long it took to draft it, what the five different sections of the draft are called, and what it says and means. Present your findings.

Discussion: Why do you think it is essential for a country to have a document such as the Declaration of Independence that states, in great detail, the intentions of its citizens and governing bodies?

CHAPTER 10: Trapped in Time

Vocabulary List: translucent, spectacle, worrisome, conviction, solidarity, poppycock, admonished, skeptical, presume, dictated, intuitive, emblematic, maturity, principle

Discussion Questions:

1. As Kat is trying to get the magic torch to work, she feels the pressure of everyone looking at her and waiting for her to make something happen. Have you ever been in a situation where you have felt that same kind of nervous pressure? Explain.

_____

_____

2. What are the most important values that the Declaration of Independence represents?

_____

_____

3. What finally made the torch work? _____

_____

_____

4. When Thomas Jefferson says, "Miss McGee, our future is in great hands if you are emblematic of the children of your era", what does he mean? _____

_____

_____

5. What lessons did Kat teach Mr. Jefferson and the others? __

_____

Activities:

Pretend that you are the author of *Kat McGee Saves America,* and, in the space below, write what you think will happen next.

_____

_____

CHAPTER 11: A New and Improved Living Museum

Vocabulary List: nimbly, reformed, wondrous, nondescript

Discussion Questions:

1. When Kat asks Thomas Jefferson about his well-being, he says that he is feeling "fit as a fiddle." What does this saying mean?

_____

_____

2. What did Rulerwink invent years after his encounter with Kat? _____

What was his reason for inventing it? _____

_____

3. What did Rulerwink learn? _____

_____

_____

Activities:

Pretend that you are Kat McGee and write thank you notes to Gram, Thomas Jefferson, Rulerwink, and JQ, thanking each of them for the lessons they taught to you throughout this great adventure.

As a class, create your own living museum. Each student should choose a historical person or event that was mentioned in the book to represent. Dress up as that person, or a person from that event, and recite dialogue indicative of that person or time. Be sure to include key facts and information to share with your peers. Present your living museum in the school library so that other classes can take a tour, and learn about America!

CHAPTER 12: Fireworks in Totsville

Vocabulary List: subdued, minions, distraught, snidely, composure, nemesis, dispersed,

Discussion Questions:

1. How did Kat McGee and Roman Rule both end up working on the Totsville Parade of Floats and Fireworks? _____

_____

_____

2. Who is Roman Rule's distant relative? _____

3. What is the overall theme of this book? _____

_____

_____

4. What was your favorite part of Kat's adventure? _____

_____

_____

5. What lesson did Kat McGee learn about the 4th of July holiday? _____

_____

_____

Activities:

Kat McGee Fact Checker: Research the following details that the author, Kristin Riddick, included in this story, and decide whether each detail is Fact or Fiction.

1. The American History Museum, where Gram takes Kat McGee and her siblings, is located at the Independence National Historical Park in Philadelphia.

2. John Quincy Adams grew up and became the 6th President of the United States.

3. The Freedom Fort, where Rulerwink holds Thomas Jefferson hostage, is a real place located outside of Philadelphia.

4. JQ got Kat McGee a dress to wear from Betsy Ross. Betsy Ross worked as a seamstress who mended uniforms.

5. JQ and Kat McGee sought out help from Paul Revere. John Quincy Adams and Paul Revere were family friends.

6. Romulus Rulerwink was the first to invent glue.

7. Life, Liberty, and the Pursuit of Romulus is a play on the phrase "Life, liberty, and the pursuit of happiness", which is a famous phrase taken directly from the Declaration of Independence. In 1776, the phrase was meant to give examples of rights that every man had been given upon birth, and lists those rights that should be protected by the government.

8. The American Revolution was almost over when the Declaration of Independence was signed.

9. Thomas Jefferson and John Adams worked together to draft the Declaration of Independence, but later campaigned against each other for the office of President of the United States.

10. The Declaration of Independence was stolen by the British in 1776 two days before it was meant to be signed.

Fact Checker Answers:

1. Fiction, the National Museum of American History is in Washington, DC.

2. Fact

3. Fiction, There is no Freedom Fort outside of Philadelphia.

4. Fact, Betsy Ross did work for an upholsterer and was married to one, her husband John Ross. She was also a seamstress who mended uniforms and was a flag maker.

5. Fiction, It is doubtful that Paul Revere ever would have had an occasion to meet John Quincy Adams.

6. Fiction, The first glue patent was issued in 1750 in Britain. It is unclear when it was first brought to the United States.

7. Fiction, at this time period, the intended meaning was for every white man, as all African Americans were not given their freedom until after the Civil War, almost 100 years later, and women were not given the right to vote until 1920.

8. Fiction, The Revolution didn't begin in earnest until after the signing of the Declaration of Independence

9. Fact, In 1800 Thomas Jefferson defeated Adams and became president. This was the first peaceful transfer of authority from one party to another in the history of the young nation.

10. Fiction, thankfully!

For more educational and character-building activities, visit beanoblekid.org

Common Core Curriculum Standards met by this Reading Guide

Grade 3:

CCSS.ELA-LITERACY.RL.3.1 Ask and answer questions to demonstrate understanding of a text, referring explicitly to the textas the basis for the answers.
CCSS.ELA-LITERACY.RL.3.3 Describe characters in a story (e.g., their traits, motivations, or feelings) and explain how theiractions contribute to the sequence of events
CCSS.ELA-LITERACY.RL.3.4 Determine the meaning of words and phrases as they are used in a text, distinguishing literalfrom nonliteral language.
CCSS.ELA-LITERACY.RL.3.6 Distinguish their own point of view from that of the narrator or those of the characters.
CCSS.ELA-LITERACY.L.3.4 Determine or clarify the meaning of unknown and multiple-meaning word and phrases based ongrade 3 reading and content, choosing flexibly from a range of strategies.
CCSS.ELA-LITERACY.L.3.4.D Use glossaries or beginning dictionaries, both print and digital, to determine or clarify theprecise meaning of key words and phrases.
CCSS.ELA-LITERACY.L.3.5 Demonstrate understanding of figurative language, word relationships and nuances in word meanings.
CCSS.ELA-LITERACY.SL.3.1 Engage effectively in a range of collaborative discussions (one-on-one, in groups, and teacherled) with diverse partners on grade 3 topics and texts, building on others' ideas and expressing their own clearly.
CCSS.ELA-LITERACY.SL.3.4 Report on a topic or text, tell a story, or recount an experience with appropriate facts andrelevant, descriptive details, speaking clearly at an understandable pace.
CCSS.ELA-Literacy.W.3.7 Conduct short research projects that build knowledge about a topic.

Grade 4:

CCSS.ELA-Literacy.RL.4.1 Refer to details and examples in a text when explaining what the text says explicitly and when drawing inferences from the text.
CCSS.ELA-Literacy.RL.4.2 Determine a theme of a story, drama, or poem from details in the text; summarize the text.
CCSS.ELA-Literacy.RL.4.3 Describe in depth a character, setting, or event in a story or drama, drawing on specific details in the text (e.g., a character's thoughts, words, or actions).
CCSS.ELA-Literacy.RL.4.4 Determine the meaning of words and phrases as they are used in a text, including those that allude to significant characters found in mythology (e.g., Herculean).
CCSS.ELA-Literacy.L.4.4 Determine or clarify the meaning of unknown and multiple-meaning words and phrases based on grade 4 reading and content, choosing flexibly from a range of strategies.
CCSS.ELA-Literacy.L.4.4.a Use context (e.g., definitions, examples, or restatements in text) as a clue to the meaning of a word or phrase.
CCSS.ELA-Literacy.L.4.4.c Consult reference materials (e.g., dictionaries, glossaries, thesauruses), both print and digital, to find the pronunciation and determine or clarify the precise meaning of key words and phrases.
CCSS.ELA-Literacy.SL.4.1 Engage effectively in a range of collaborative discussions (one-on-one, in groups, and teacher-led) with diverse partners on *grade 4 topics and texts*, building on others' ideas and expressing their own clearly.
CCSS.ELA-Literacy.SL.4.4 Report on a topic or text, tell a story, or recount an experience in an organized manner, using appropriate facts and relevant, descriptive details to support main ideas or themes; speak clearly at an understandable pace.
CCSS.ELA-Literacy.W.4.2 Write informative/explanatory texts to examine a topic and convey ideas and information clearly.

Grade 5:

CCSS.ELA-Literacy.RL.5.2
Determine a theme of a story, drama, or poem from details in the text, including how characters in a story or drama respond to challenges or how the speaker in a poem reflects upon a topic; summarize the text.

CCSS.ELA-Literacy.RL.5.3
Compare and contrast two or more characters, settings, or events in a story or drama, drawing on specific details in the text (e.g., how characters interact).

CCSS.ELA-Literacy.RL.5.4
Determine the meaning of words and phrases as they are used in a text, including figurative language such as metaphors and similes.

CCSS.ELA-Literacy.L.5.4
Determine or clarify the meaning of unknown and multiple-meaning words and phrases based on grade 5 reading and content, choosing flexibly from a range of strategies.

CCSS.ELA-Literacy.L.5.4.c
Consult reference materials (e.g., dictionaries, glossaries, thesauruses), both print and digital, to find the pronunciation and determine or clarify the precise meaning of key words and phrases.

CCSS.ELA-Literacy.L.5.5
Demonstrate understanding of figurative language, word relationships, and nuances in word meanings.

CCSS.ELA-Literacy.L.5.5.a
Interpret figurative language, including similes and metaphors, in context.

CCSS.ELA-Literacy.SL.5.1
Engage effectively in a range of collaborative discussions (one-on-one, in groups, and teacher-led) with diverse partners on *grade 5 topics and texts*, building on others' ideas and expressing their own clearly.

CCSS.ELA-Literacy.SL.5.4
Report on a topic or text or present an opinion, sequencing ideas logically and using appropriate facts and relevant, descriptive details to support main ideas or themes; speak clearly at an understandable pace.

CCSS.ELA-Literacy.SL.5.5
Include multimedia components (e.g., graphics, sound) and visual displays in presentations when appropriate to enhance the development of main ideas or themes.

CCSS.ELA-Literacy.W.5.2
Write informative/explanatory texts to examine a topic and convey ideas and information clearly.
CCSS.ELA-Literacy.W.5.7
Conduct short research projects that use several sources to build knowledge through investigation of different aspects of a topic.
CCSS.ELA-Literacy.W.5.9
Draw evidence from literary or informational texts to support analysis, reflection, and research.
CCSS.ELA-Literacy.W.5.9.a
Apply *grade 5 Reading standards* to literature (e.g., "Compare and contrast two or more characters, settings, or events in a story or a drama, drawing on specific details in the text [e.g., how characters interact]").

Authors: National Governors Association Center for Best Practices, Council of Chief State School Officers

Title: Common Core State Standards

Publisher: National Governors Association Center for Best Practices, Council of Chief State School Officers, Washington D.C.

12301723R00090

Made in the USA
San Bernardino, CA
12 June 2014